TEEN
FIC Alexander

KATE SABLOWSKY PARANORMAL INVESTIGATOR SERIES

Book One

SHE'S STILL HERE

CAITLIN ALEXANDER

BOOKS THAT MATTER

To Ian, Lexi, and Landon

Prologue

A door slammed, shattering the stillness of the empty Ravendale Middle School.

I heard it from the seventh-grade hallway, the sound bouncing off the lockers on either side of me. From any outside entrance, it would only take a person twenty seconds to reach the chem lab where *it* happened.

I shot to attention, punching the record button on my camera as firmly as I could. I shoved it in my backpack and left the compartment unzipped. Good video wasn't necessary, but the audio had to be clear.

I kept my eyes glued toward the direction of the sound. Armed with only a softball bat, I inched backward and positioned myself in front of my friend, spreading my arms wide to shield her from the approaching evil. Pounding footsteps filled the hall.

The only other movement came from particles of dust floating around us, made visible by a single fluorescent light above. The rest of the hallway was dark. I shuddered, thinking of what was about to emerge from that darkness.

"We'll be okay. Everything is going to be okay," I whispered, not believing my own words for even a second.

The steps drew closer. They belonged to a murderer—a killer who had stolen the life of a child and was now on the way to meet us.

Chapter One

The walls of my new bedroom were stark white, like that place Michael Myers escaped from in the beginning of *Halloween*. It didn't help that they formed a perfect square too.

Great. A cell.

Mom said the wide-plank chestnut floors were original to the house, built in the 1920s. Those were something, at least. She'd had a handyman sand and restain them before we moved in, so they'd look darker and more polished. But I still planned to cover them up with my black fuzzy rug to stress to Mom how little I wanted to be there.

I dug in the back pocket of my jeans and pulled out my phone. With a click, I snapped a picture of the bleak white cube that was my room. I dropped the photo in the text thread with Bailey, my best friend back home in Illinois. More "home" than this place anyway. I rolled my eyes as I typed.

Here we go again.

Sent. I hoped she would respond right away and not make me wonder if she'd already found better friends to replace me. Couldn't blame her though. I was the one who'd left.

My four-poster bed, mattress, and bookshelf were all that had made it off the moving truck into my cell so far. The room was stuffy, which wasn't shocking for the second-to-last week of August. I flung my heavy purple duffel bag onto my naked mattress. It was packed with all of my favorite old movies, some on DVD, some on videotape. Everyone streamed the movies they watched, but I'd always hung onto the hard copies of the classics.

I picked up my VHS copy of *The Shining* and placed it on my shelf, a tinge dusty from the move. My horror films deserved the prime spot in this room, like they had in all the others. These worn-out cases had sat on this shelf in so many different rooms. They deserved better. *I* deserved better.

My phone buzzed with Bailey's response. A face-palm emoji. *Glad we are in agreement.*

"Kate, can you move your bags out of the entryway?" Mom's deep, authoritative voice echoed up the stairs. "The movers want to get your desk off the truck!"

All of northeast Iowa would know that voice before long.

My mom was *that* Maria Silver. Except Silver wasn't even her real name. Our last name was Sablowksy, but that was never punchy enough for TV. As an evening news anchor, she went by Silver, her mom's—my bubbe's—maiden name. Everywhere we lived, people recognized her at the store. I'd always just been "Maria Silver's daughter," quiet and awkward with dishwater-blond, frizzy hair.

I played along. The truth was, my mom was pretty cool, minus all the moving for higher-ranking TV jobs. It had always been the two of us. My dad had never been around, but I didn't let that wreck my childhood or anything. Mom was smart—funny, too, when she wasn't talking about the news. It didn't hurt that she pretty much let me watch whatever movies I wanted, even though I was only twelve. She knew I always told her the truth about the important stuff in life and kept up good grades. Also, I'd gotten fairly decent at making my own dinners, so she didn't need to come home from work on dinner breaks.

"You're a keeper," she always told me. She was too.

Even so, I couldn't believe it when she'd said we were moving to Ravendale, Iowa, after only two years in Peoria, Illinois, where Mom had been the weekend news anchor. When the opportunity came to take the main weeknight anchor gig in Ravendale, she said it was too good to pass up.

"C'mon, Kate, I'll have weekends free!" she'd practically begged. "We can go on hikes and take short trips, just like we've always talked about. You know I've never had weekends off before."

I'd objected, but she was like a dog with a bone. Before I knew it, there were commercials airing, welcoming Maria Silver to the Iowa airwaves.

Ravendale was a tiny town about thirty miles south of the Minnesota border with more farm fields than roads. I thought of that movie *Field of Dreams*. Mom had made me watch that ahead of our move, because it took place in Iowa. The guy created his own baseball field in his backyard because there was literally nothing else to do there. And that's where I found myself. Same spot, just short a baseball field. My first day of seventh grade was the following day with kids who thought this little farm community was normal.

BOOM.

"This good, ma'am?" one of the movers asked as he plopped my desk against the wall opposite my bed. I smirked, picturing Mom hearing the sound and worrying about the precious floors.

"Sure, thanks," I managed, squelching another quick wave of self-pity.

"It's all coming together, kiddo!" Mom said as she walked past the mover and into my room. She darted a glance at where he had slammed the desk. It must have been okay because her gaze returned to me. She didn't have any of her TV makeup on, but her perfect skin glowed. Sometime earlier that day, she'd pulled her unwashed blond curls in a ponytail and still managed to look cute. "We've just got to track down the box that has our sheets and comforters. If nothing else, I know where I packed the towels. Those could do."

She winked as she flopped onto her back on my bare mattress.

"Hilarious," I replied with the flattest tone possible.

"You look just like your bubbe when you get mad, you know that? Big brown eyes. Your lower lip puckered out. It's cute." Mom laughed, poking her finger at my mouth. I pushed her finger away and rolled those brown eyes again. "Actually, speaking of Bubbe, I thought she could help you get settled in."

I blinked, confused. We'd lost Bubbe about four years ago.

Mom dug into her jeans pocket and fished out a thin, gold chain. A single charm dangled from it. I recognized the charm as *chai*, the Hebrew word for life. It was in almost every family photo, because Bubbe never took her bracelet off. Mom gently tugged at my right arm, to pull me down next to her, and fastened the bracelet's claw clip on my wrist. Bracelets never fit my small, bony wrists, but this one was perfect.

"'Life's not just the here and now,'" Mom recalled with a smile. "Bubbe always said that. I know moving so often at your age sucks, but let's make the most of it. If Iowa isn't right for us, we'll land somewhere else eventually. But you have to believe me; I feel it in my bones that this place is going to be different."

I didn't lift my gaze from Bubbe's bracelet, gently examining the charm I'd seen so many times before. Mom started lightly scratching my back, like she used to do when I was little and got jumpy after watching a scary movie.

I took a deep breath and replayed the goal I'd set for myself in my mind: to survive the few years of Mom's TV contract before we could move somewhere meaningful. Somewhere I could go to film festivals. Somewhere I could make a difference.

"Ravendale, Iowa. Where Kate Sablowsky's dreams come true," I mocked.

My sarcasm got a chuckle from Mom.

I didn't know it then, but I was dead wrong. Our new hometown was going to be where my *nightmares* would come true.

The Sablowsky girls were in Ravendale for an important reason. It wasn't for Mom to anchor the news.

Chapter Two

By the time the sun came up Monday morning, about half of my stuff had made it into drawers and the closet. I kicked a box out of my way as I trudged to the bathroom, practically still asleep.

I settled on a black T-shirt and dark jeans with small rips at the knees. I wanted to fit in with the Iowa kids for my first day, but I drew the line at flannel. I'd seen one kid wearing that on our drive into town.

I even spent a little time with Mom's TV-grade hair straightener, smoothing out some of my frizz. By the time I was done, my hair looked alright, falling just below my shoulders.

CLICK.

"First day, kiddo!" Mom lowered her smartphone camera, then leaned against the bathroom door frame . Her tired voice did its best to sound chipper before giving way to a yawn. "You look great."

"Mom!" I protested, smoothing out one last fly-away hair.

"Let me just throw on some shorts and grab us some granola bars." Fake chipper again. "Then, we can head out!"

Mom pocketed her phone and rubbed her eyes. As an evening news anchor, mornings were not her thing. That was how our deal began in Peoria last year. Most mornings (when the temperature wasn't below freezing), I got myself ready, then texted Mom to let her know when I'd made it safely to school. In exchange, my rules weren't as strict as other kids'. She'd initially fought me on the idea, but after a week of being able to sleep past nine, she warmed up to it.

"Actually, Mom? Could you... *not* come?" I closed one eye, bracing myself for her reaction. My voice sounded harsher than I'd intended.

Mom had turned away from the bathroom, but she whipped around again to face me.

"And miss your first day? Yeah, right. Good try." She grinned and tousled the section of hair I'd just fixed. I smoothed my hair back into place and inhaled a breath of courage to give it to her straight.

"It's not that I don't want you with me. I do. But this move stinks enough on its own. Just once, let me start a school year without the 'Look, it's Maria Silver' spectacle. At least on day one."

She blinked at me for a moment, before releasing a tiny smile. "Hurtful but fair," she mumbled. Her expression told me she was joking.

Mom didn't fully let me off the hook though. She forced me to pose for an official "back to school" photo with my backpack on and give her an unnecessarily long hug. I knew she'd be back asleep before I made it out the front door. Of course, her phone would be on its loudest setting, so she'd hear the ding of my "I arrived safe and sound" text.

The maps app put the walk at about a mile, and the temperature had already climbed into the mid-70s. I was sure at least some of my frizz had returned by the time I approached the redbrick building of my new school. A quick check of myself on selfie mode confirmed that.

Next, I opened my text thread with Mom.

> Got eaten by ravenous wolves. Wish me luck.
> Love you.

No more than a few seconds later, my phone lit up with a four-leaf-clover emoji in response. The exchange was on-brand for us.

Gray stone steps led up to four glass doors. It wasn't only my first day. It was the first day of fall semester for all of Ravendale Middle School. Mom had gone on and on about how thrilled she was with the timing of our move.

Maybe she'd be less thrilled if she saw this place.

The school looked dated. It had that kind of cream-paneled ceiling that was probably packed with asbestos. Mustard-colored lockers, not from this decade, lined the hall.

The front office loomed to the left of the main doors. The school secretary had to have been in her seventies. She wore baby-blue-framed glasses that hung on a beaded string around her neck. She delivered what I assumed to be the standard "Welcome to Ravendale Middle blah blah blah" speech, then pointed in the general direction of the seventh-grade hallway.

I found my way to locker 117, two right turns away. This wing of the school appeared to be newer than the area I'd passed through. Fresher ivory paint and more modern (non-mustard) lockers. I bet that peeved the other classes.

"That's her, I think," whispered a blond girl to her friend a few lockers down. They quickly turned away when I looked up. Even without Mom accompanying me to school, it seemed word of "Maria Silver's daughter" had already spread at Ravendale. I wished Bailey was with me.

"Let's try to keep it down, shall we?" called out a stern, older voice over the buzz of student chatter. A teacher with gold-framed glasses leaned out of his classroom door. He had gelled gray hair circling a glaring bald patch on top. His short-sleeved, white dress shirt was starched, ironed, and perfect. His tie was knotted just right. *The school stickler.* He seemed easy to pin.

He uttered one final "Humpfh" as he walked back into his room and closed his door with purpose. His reaction struck me as a little much for the first day back, but I didn't know the guy.

I pulled my class schedule out of my "Welcome to Raven-dale" folder. I noted the name outside his classroom, then checked the sheet.

Mr. Davis, Chemistry. It appeared I'd get to know him shortly.

I tossed my backpack inside my locker and grabbed a note-book and pencil bag for my first class. The hallway was emptying, so the first bell had to be soon. I had English first period, which was a relief. I always enjoyed English. You sort of had to enjoy reading and writing to be into film.

RINGGGG.

The bell sounded as I walked through the doorway to Mrs. Marsh's room.

Then, it hit me like a wave. A chill that ran all the way down my spine, shooting goosebumps up through my skin.

What is happening? Am I that nervous for my first day?

"Hello, dear! Why, you must be Kate!" a friendly-faced woman with brown, graying curls said as she scurried toward me. She was long and lean. Her dangly earrings chimed along the way. "I'm Marilyn Marsh. Well, Mrs. Marsh to you, I suppose. I can't wait to watch your mom on the news tonight. It's too excit-ing! Sit anywhere you'd like, dear. We'll get started momentarily."

Between the cold blast and the energetic welcome, I'd almost overlooked the classroom itself. Bright and beautiful colors filled the space, from the drapes to the inspirational quotes on the walls. Even the whiteboard had a rainbow array of markers to choose from.

All of the seats were spoken for, except for one in the very back row. In fact, there were only two desks that far back. One was claimed by a fair-skinned brunette, with a gray sweater buttoned all the way up to her neck. A crisp, white collar poked out the top. She blended into the background in a way I imagined I might too. She struck me as less annoying than a few other girls, wearing color-coordinated flannel shirts over their crop tops, in the class.

Of course, it has to be flannel.

"Welcome back, everyone!" Mrs. Marsh sang, as she brought her hands to her cheeks. "My, it's so good to see your faces again. I trust you all had a very relaxing summer. Of course, I probably saw most of you at the diner at some point or other."

Oy. The *diner? As in, there's just one?*

I fought the urge to slam my forehead on my desk.

"I hope you all had a chance to read Anne Frank's *The Diary of a Young Girl* over your break," she continued. "A stunning, heartbreaking text. But before we dive in, I'd like for everyone to turn and give a warm welcome to our new student, Kate Sablowsky. Or should I say, Silver?"

Mrs. Marsh giggled.

I couldn't even be mad. She seemed so genuinely excited.

"Sablowsky. Err, Kate is good," I said, with a small wave to all of the eyes staring back at me.

"I say Silver, because her mom is *the* Maria Silver, our new TV anchor on KTRD. Kate, I imagine you want to be a journalist, just like your mom." Mrs. Marsh glowed.

I didn't want to burst her bubble.

"Umm, I'm actually more into film," I muttered, unsure

anyone else would care. My cheeks flushed. "I think I'd like to be a filmmaker someday."

"Well, that's splendid too," said Mrs. Marsh. "If you didn't have a chance to read the assigned book over the summer, dear, I completely understand."

I cut her off as gently as I could. "That's okay. I've actually read it."

"Oh?" Her hands were still clasped together with glee. She brought them to her other cheek. "Assigned reading at your last school perhaps?"

"Not exactly. It's one of the most well-known books about the Holocaust, and I'm Jewish. My mom makes me read most of that stuff. You know, awareness of where I came from and all that." I got quieter as I finished my sentence through semi-gritted teeth. I sank an inch lower in my seat.

None of my classmates so much as blinked.

Great, now I'm Maria Silver's daughter and probably the only Jewish kid in class.

"Wonderful, dear," Mrs. Marsh said, smiling but skimming over what I'd said. "Let's get started."

"You'll get used to her," whispered the sweater girl next to me, her gaze never leaving Mrs. Marsh's face. "She strikes you as a giddy Mary Poppins, but she really is sweet. And a stickler for grammar, which keeps you on your toes."

"I see it," I whispered back, wanting to laugh, but following her lead of staring straight ahead. "She's just missing the flying umbrella."

The sweater girl's eyes grew wider. The corners of her lips rose ever so slightly, offering me the warmest smile possible during a lecture about a Holocaust text. "I'm Jane, by the way," she said in her hushed tone.

"Kate," I responded. A red-headed boy in the row ahead of us shot me a confused look over his shoulder. He probably thought it was dumb I was introducing myself after my class introduction.

When the bell eventually rang to signal the end of class, all of the students gathered their belongings and shipped off to second period. A cluster of them hurried out the door, and Mrs. Marsh followed, her voice echoing into the hallway as she reiterated the night's homework assignment.

Only Jane and I were left, collecting our things.

"I don't want to smother you on your first day, but I know this place pretty well if you have any questions," Jane offered. "It's got to be way lamer than wherever you came from."

I appreciated her dry remark. It made me feel more at home, if that's even possible in Iowa.

"Yeah, actually," I said, turning toward her. "What do you know about that grinch, Mr. Davis?"

"Ah." She nodded knowingly. "I don't think he's so bad. Teaches chemistry. A smart guy and super helpful if you ask. A lot of people joke that he's a robot. He's not a, you know, 'people' person." Jane used her fingers to make air quotes. "See you around?"

"Yeah, see ya." I gave a half-smile, as I headed for the door. This was the first time someone ever struck up a conversation with me on my first day at a new school that wasn't about my mom. It was a pleasant surprise.

I turned around and offered a wave. Jane waved back, standing at her desk.

Chapter Three

After English, I had math class. My least favorite subject. Mr. Smith seemed nice enough though. He was heavyset with combed-back blond hair, sort of like the T-Birds in *Grease*. He didn't single me out as the new kid, which I appreciated. He went over expectations for the year, while resting a hand on the giant cowboy buckle on his belt.

Very Iowa.

Next came social studies, then lunch.

With my tray steeped high with soggy-looking chicken nuggets, I trudged slowly past the long, white lunch tables, keeping an eye out for Jane. A few kids here and there whispered to each other, probably about the "Maria Silver's daughter" bit. I pretended not to see. Unfortunately, I didn't see Jane anywhere.

I opted to sit at a table in the furthest corner by myself. Between deep dives into a pool of ketchup, I looked up *The Diary of a Young Girl* on my phone and refreshed my memory on the details.

After lunch, it was time for chemistry. I generally felt the same about science as I did about math.

Mr. Davis's room was spotless and bordered on empty. There were no family photos, no posters on the walls. Not even a display of the periodic table. Mr. Davis's desk sat in the front right corner of the room. At a glance, I spotted a computer, a landline phone, a small, neat stack of papers, and a white mug filled with pens.

His desk faced four long, rectangular lab tables with black countertops. Each table had goggles, a few glass beakers, and a Bunsen burner. I knew enough from movies to recognize them. They were gas burners that teachers and students used for lab experiments.

Mr. Davis stood before the class, his hands clasped firmly in front of him. His white dress shirt was somehow completely free of wrinkles, despite half the day being gone. He turned his head in the same rhythmic way to observe each student entering the lab. He didn't greet anyone, just scrutinized.

Totally a robot. Jane and the others were right.

When everyone was seated, he spoke at last, skipping over any welcome message.

"We need to start with solids, liquids, and gasses," he stated matter-of-factly. "Any gas jokes won't be tolerated."

That last comment caused some of the boys to snicker. Mr. Davis shot a glare at them, and they instantly went silent.

"You're sitting across from your permanent lab partner for the semester," he continued. "You may quickly and quietly introduce yourselves if you don't know each other already."

The boy in a Nirvana T-shirt across from me swiveled around on his stool. He had brown hair that kicked out around his neck and a face full of freckles.

"I'm Sam," he began at the exact moment I opened my mouth to speak. He stopped and his hazel eyes grew big. "Oh, I'm sorry, go ahead."

His freckles became a bit more pronounced as his cheeks

flushed.

"It's okay," I said. "I'm Kate."

A weird silence fell between us, neither wanting to speak over the other. Sam looked down as he picked at a hangnail. After another few beats, he peeked up at me.

"I heard you're the weather lady's daughter. That's pretty cool," he blurted, still avoiding direct eye contact.

I shrugged, trying to put him at ease. "Technically, *news* lady's daughter, but it's all the same."

"Cool," Sam said again. He paused and shook his bangs out of his eyes, peering around the room and continuing to tug on his hangnail. It took him a few seconds to find the confidence to string together more than a few words. "Anyway, I was the new kid last year. My dad moved us here when he took a foreman job at the Jefferson Foods plant. It can really suck, but at least there's someone else who knows what you're going through. I won't make things worse and be a crappy lab partner."

I smiled. He was a bit awkward, but he seemed friendly. Good with me.

Mr. Davis continued speaking before I could respond.

"Open your textbooks to page 37 and read the chapter quietly for the remainder of class. We'll have a quiz tomorrow before starting any experiments."

Wow, somebody call the fun police.

Sam shot me a look that suggested he thought the same thing. I'd never had a teacher use the first day of school as a silent reading period. Mr. Davis didn't wait for any questions. He turned on his heels and zipped to his desk, then began tapping on his keyboard.

As I flipped the pages of my textbook, I couldn't help but feel like someone was watching me. I was the new kid, so that wasn't unlikely. I glanced around, but everyone's eyes were on their books.

Chapter Four

Smoke filled my lungs as I gasped for air. I coughed as I looked back over my shoulder. A scream escaped my mouth as a sea of red and orange surrounded me. A massive fire licked at what appeared to be tables and stools mere feet away, the heat inching closer and closer. I didn't know where I was, but I didn't have time to figure it out. Something made of glass on one of the tables burst, casting shards across the room. I raised an arm to block my eyes. I had only seconds to escape. Black, billowing smoke filled the room, making it difficult to see. I searched the area around me for any possible way out.

To my right: a door. I hurled myself toward it, dodging something circular and engulfed in flames that fell from the ceiling.

I reached for the handle, warm to the touch but not yet scalding. It wouldn't turn. With every ounce of strength I had, I pounded my fists against the door. My screams erupted between coughs. There was no air left in the room. Someone had to hear me.

"HELP! PLEASE! HELP ME!"

Tears poured from my eyes. My fists throbbed as they whaled

against the door. I bent down, bringing my eyes to the narrow glass window in the door that looked out to the hallway.

No one was coming.

* * *

I SHOT UP TO A SEATED POSITION IN MY BED, SWEAT CIRCLES on my red pajama top. I massaged my throat, sore from coughing, as my heart thundered in my chest.

It had been a dream.

Why did everything feel so real?

That kind of reaction was embarrassing for a girl who had watched her share of scary movies. Even my nightmares after watching *First Full Moon* for the first time didn't measure up to this, and everyone knew werewolves were the freakiest.

My door opened a crack and I froze, terrified my nightmare wasn't over.

"Kiddo, are you sick? I just got home and I heard you coughing from downstairs." Mom shuffled into my room and sat next to me on the bed.

I glanced at my phone. It was 11:13 P.M. Mom's newscast ended about forty-five minutes ago. I grabbed her into a fierce bear hug.

"Not sick, Mom. Just the worst dream ever. I was trapped in a room that was on fire. I couldn't get out, and no one came to help me."

I knew how corny that sounded coming from me.

"Ugh, awful. I'm so sorry. Was your first day at school that bad?" she asked, scratching my back the way she does. "Mom's here now, and I have a fire extinguisher under the kitchen sink."

There was a twinge of humor in her final phrase to make me feel better. I sighed. No matter how much Iowa stunk, at least I had her.

Caitlin Alexander

"Hey," Mom said, her tone a bit more serious. "Do you ever have dreams about people who have passed away?"

My eyes narrowed. "No, why?"

Crickets chirped outside, cutting through the silence as Mom drew a deep breath.

"I think you might finally be old enough to hear this." She scooted an inch closer. "Bubbe had a special gift. She could see people, hear people. People who aren't here anymore. Do you know what I'm talking about?"

I'd seen that kind of thing play out in countless scary movies over the years but never in real life. Never in my family. "Sounds equal parts dope and terrifying," I joked.

Mom chuckled, continuing to trace my back. "You need to come crash with me? My door is always open."

"I'm not five, Mom," I said, pulling away as I remembered how sweaty I'd gotten. "I'll be okay. I love you."

"You're a keeper, kiddo. I love you more." As Mom walked to the door, her perfect TV curls barely moved, held intact by a helmet of hair spray.

I took a deep breath, then nestled under my blankets to give sleep another try. I glanced down at the bracelet on my wrist as I cuddled my comforter. The moonlight glistened off Bubbe's charm.

Chai. Life's not just the here and now.

Chapter Five

I took a hot shower the next morning, standing still under the warm water for way longer than necessary. I let it wash away everything I'd experienced the night before. I needed to be ready for the day ahead because teachers always started heaping on the homework on day two.

Before heading downstairs, I grabbed a T-shirt from a pile in my drawer and then threw my hair in a messy ponytail. Mom wouldn't be up yet, after her shift and probably an episode of *Real Housewives* or two. But that's what our "I'm still alive" text arrangement was for.

I packed myself a turkey sub, chips, and apple for lunch, then filled my water bottle. No need to eat cafeteria food two days in a row. I locked the front door and walked the mile to school, arriving about ten minutes before the bell. The temperature was already toasty.

When I arrived on school grounds, I shot Mom my text.

Abducted by aliens. It's been nice knowing you.

My phone lit up seconds later but without any emojis this time.

> You know you're the worst, right?

It was nice to know she loved me.

I opened my locker and emptied out everything from my backpack, including my copy of *The Diary of a Young Girl* that had taken me about an hour to find last night. I should've figured Mom would have it in a box labeled "Jewish stuff."

So her.

As students passed me headed to their first-period classrooms, I realized which shirt I'd thrown on that morning. My *First Full Moon* movie poster T-shirt drew a few judgy looks from a pack of girls in matching flannels and crop tops.

Again, with the flannel and crop tops.

I wasn't ashamed of the fact that *First Full Moon* was one of my favorite scary movies, but I *was* ashamed of the fact I'd outed myself as a horror/werewolf movie nerd on the second day of school. I kept my eyes down for the most part but snuck a few peeks here and there, hoping to catch sight of Jane. I wasn't about to unload my nightmare (or my fashion insecurities) on someone I'd just met, but I figured it would be comforting to see a friendly face.

RINGGGG.

I strode through the door to Mrs. Marsh's room and, again, that overwhelming chill encircled me. It took my breath away.

For crying out loud, someone needs to check the air conditioning.

Mrs. Marsh wasn't at her post behind her desk yet. The first several rows of desks were empty. But as I turned left to head for the back row, I saw that familiar brown bob, neatly styled and tucked behind two ears.

Jane wore the same gray sweater buttoned all the way up to her neck. The familiar white collar peeked out. Her head was down, and her pencil wiggled in her hand as she worked. Her chemistry book sat open beside her.

Crap, was there an assignment I'd missed?

"Hey, Jane," I said as I plopped down into my seat.

Jane's cool blue eyes raised from her notebook and seemed to warm when they met mine. "This place didn't scare you away after all, huh? Welcome back."

I sighed. "Not yet anyway. But you've got me worried," I said, gesturing at her chemistry work. "I didn't know we had any chem homework beyond that in-class reading to get ready for today's quiz."

Other students began to filter into the classroom and take their seats.

"Oh, we don't," Jane said, lowering her voice as the room filled. "I like science. I like chemistry. It's just—science doesn't always like me. I've always dreamt of going to med school, so I keep studying. I give myself extra assignments sometimes."

"Med school?" I said, impressed. "Wow, that's great."

I decided to give her a pass on the nerdy extra-homework bit. I followed her lead and whispered too. A blond girl in the row ahead looked back with a confused expression as she sat down. I wasn't sure what her deal was.

I wondered if maybe Jane was banking on big scholarships to someday help her get to college. Did her family maybe struggle with money and that's why she had to wear the same outfit two days in a row? It obviously wasn't my business, and well-intentioned or not, I wasn't about to ask.

"Cool shirt, by the way," Jane whispered as a grinning Mrs. Marsh floated into the room. "I mean, is that a movie? I haven't seen it, but it looks cool."

I nodded and opened my mouth to give her a recap of the plot when the human sunshine at the front of the class sang out.

"Happy Tuesday, my sweets!" Mrs. Marsh wore a purple shawl like a cape, dramatically draped over her shoulder. Rainbow earrings that said "Be Kind" danced above her shoulders. "Today, we are going to employ some critical thinking!"

I got the impression she might segue back into the art of the comma or something, but I was wrong.

"In *The Diary of a Young Girl*, we learned about the Frank family and others hiding from the Nazis in a building annex. Six helpers, who were friends of Anne's father, kept them fed and informed. This selfless action could have gotten them arrested or worse. In fact, some of them *did* get in trouble. Today, I want you to think of another example of a selfless action in a book, movie, or television show. It can be fiction or nonfiction. Then, write a paper about why that person or character made that choice. Was it about right vs. wrong? Personal obligation? Oh, I can't wait to read your thoughts!"

My ears perked up. Anything to do with movies was fine by me.

"And, of course, I'll go through your essays with my trusty red pen for perfect punctuation," Mrs. Marsh added with a smile.

The words felt like a threat, but she made it sound like a fun challenge. I was up for it.

"I'll give you the next five or so minutes to start brainstorming ideas in your notebooks. You may write the essay yourself or work with a partner. Why is that, class?"

Mrs. Marsh raised her right hand to her ear.

"Because proofreading is important," the students droned in unison.

Everyone except me anyway. I made a mental note of the response for future reference.

Jane shot me a smile. Maybe she knew I'd get a kick out of that.

"Would you want to be partners?" she whispered, staring ahead.

"Sure," I responded, doing the same. "You can come by my house after school to work on the essay if you'd like. My mom will be at work, but she won't care."

"If it's okay with you, it'd actually be easier for me to meet here, at school. Maybe in the library or something?" Embarrassment seemed to twinge Jane's voice.

I wondered why, but I told her that was fine. We agreed to meet in the library at 2:45, following last period.

When class ended, I waved to Jane as I left. She returned my smile, standing at her desk. I could feel her eyes on me as I walked away.

Chapter Six

M r. Davis was a man of his word. Our quizzes on solids, liquids, and gasses were waiting for us at our chem stations when we walked into the lab that afternoon. Mr. Davis meandered down the rows, keeping a sharp eye on us as we took the quiz. He absentmindedly smoothed his long, black tie over his maroon-colored dress shirt with one hand. His pants had that cliché-looking dad crease down the front, and his glasses were perfectly smudge-free.

I knew the answers, or at least I thought I did. I'd find out later after he let his red pen run loose on our stack of papers, neatly piled on his desk.

Mr. Davis then passed out a water bottle, a packet of Alka Seltzer tablets, and a balloon to each lab station.

"You'll all get to take part in a quick-and-easy experiment," Mr. Davis droned. "You and your partner will follow the steps I'm about to outline verbally. Listen closely, as I will not repeat them."

The whole point, he explained, was to differentiate between solids, liquids, and gasses.

I'd done the same experiment in elementary school, but I was not about to cross Mr. Davis. He instructed us to drink half of the water from our water bottles, then drop two tablets into the water that remained. We had to then attach the balloon to the top of the bottle. The combination would create a gas and cause the balloon to inflate.

Sam unscrewed the cap from the water bottle. With a small shrug, he extended his arm, offering the bottle to me.

"Ha, no thanks," I said. "You go for it."

Sam tossed the bottle back with gusto. When about half of the water was gone, he returned the bottle to the table.

"That's a sick shirt," he said, wiping his mouth with the back of his hand. "I swear, when the wolf ate those twins, I almost puked."

My jaw dropped.

"You like *First Full Moon*?"

"Duh. My brother got me into it," he said as he fumbled with the tablets' packaging. He tried and failed to tear it a few times, then changed the subject. "Have you made any friends yet?"

"You mean here?" I asked. I'd been texting Bailey a bit but didn't feel the need to share that. It sounded too sad that my only real friend was hours away. "There is a girl named Jane in my English class who seems alright."

Sam stopped struggling with the wrapping and wrinkled his nose, appearing puzzled.

"Jane? She's a seventh grader?"

I grabbed the tablet packet from him and tore it open with one pull. "Yeah, she's a seventh grader. You don't know her?"

"No, but I still don't know everyone here. The new-kid thing sticks a while." Sam grabbed the deflated blue balloon and opened it at the bottom. "You ready?"

I nodded.

His reaction to my mention of Jane sent confusion rippling

through me. They had to have at least one class together. Maybe the other kids shared my first impression of Jane—that she easily blended into the background.

I didn't push it and turned my attention to the experiment. I dropped the two tablets into the bottle. Sam swooped in with the balloon and attached it to the top. We watched our balloon inflate. Not exciting.

"Lame, but we didn't fail. So, that's something," Sam said with another shrug.

His honesty made me laugh. I had to agree with him.

Mr. Davis spent the remainder of class showing us a video on the states of matter. He corrected our quizzes while we watched.

When the bell rang at last, Mr. Davis robotically stood up from his desk and strode to the door with his lanyard in hand. He stepped into the hallway and held the door as the students filed past. I waved to both Sam and Mr. Davis as I left. Mr. Davis didn't make eye contact or say a word. Out of curiosity, I watched from my locker as the last student exited the lab. Mr. Davis switched the light off and thrust a key from his lanyard into the lock. With a flick of the wrist, he locked the lab and began marching down the hall.

What a weird guy. Does he ever let loose?

The rest of the day flew by. I only needed to check my school map twice. When the final bell rang, I grabbed my backpack and all of my homework from my locker before heading to meet Jane in the library. Most of the other seventh graders had cleared out for the day. It was like a game to see who could be out the door first.

A white piece of paper was taped to the library's wooden double doors with a message scribbled in thick black marker:

Sorry, kids

I have an early afternoon appointment today so the library is closed! Be a Dahl and don't get your Dickens in a twist until I see you Thoreau.

Make it a great day!!

—Mr. E

The dots on the double exclamation point were fashioned into eyes on a smiley face. I figured the peppy author had to be the school's librarian.

Despite the note, I was surprised to see the door was not "closed"—it was cracked open. Peeking through the crack, I could see most of the lights were shut off, but a row of warm white lights illuminated a large study table where Jane sat with her chem book open in front of her. I glanced around me then stepped inside.

It was the only room in the school with stained-glass windows, which was actually kind of beautiful in the midafternoon light. The panes showed a fall day in Ravendale. A tractor plowed a field with a classic red silo and barn in the distance.

Pretty, but too Iowa.

Another chill awakened my goosebumps. I rubbed my arms, irritated at the school's wonky air-conditioning system.

From floor to tall ceilings, colorful books lined the massive shelves, labeled by genre. The room smelled the way libraries often do—of well-loved, old pages and a hint of dust. Among the rows, I spotted a small DVD section. I made a mental note to check them out sometime, but I figured there wouldn't be many horror films available to check out from a middle school.

Jane's pencil scrawled away on a notebook next to her chemistry book. The room was silent enough to hear a pin drop.

"You can take the girl out of chem class..." I began.

Jane, catching my drift, responded, "But you can't take the chem class out of the girl. I know, I know. It's endless."

"Hey, I think it's cool you're taking school so seriously and already know what you want to do with your life," I said as I plopped into a hard wooden chair. "My mom says she was like that at our age. She was a reporter for her school newspaper and got detention for sneaking into the cafeteria to dig up dirt about cleanliness standards for a story."

Jane's blue eyes twinkled. "Your mom sounds awesome. I guess I don't need to tell you that though. Everyone already does. You seem great too."

I'd been needing to hear that, especially since moving to Ravendale. I let a second of silence pass, appreciating her kindness.

"The note on the door said the library is closed," I finally said. "Do you think it's okay for us to be in here?"

Jane put her pencil down, closed her chem book, and looked

up with a smile. "From what I've noticed of Mr. E, he won't mind."

I returned Jane's smile. She didn't strike me as much of a rule-breaker, but she knew the school better than I did. I wanted to know more about her.

"So, what do your parents do? Are you as embarrassed as I am half the time?" I asked, simply making conversation.

Jane smirked. "My dad is a banker. My mom is a nurse, but you'd think she made her living by calling me Buttercup in public places. Sooo embarrassing."

I could relate. "Mine calls me kiddo. Just as bad." That got a giggle out of Jane.

"What do you say we dig in?" I asked. "Any ideas of films we could write about?"

"I don't know. You seem to be the expert on that kind of stuff. If I told you the last movie I remember seeing, you'd make fun of me." She tucked her chin in embarrassment.

"I will not. What was it?"

Jane eyed me for a second, seeming to weigh the risk of telling her secret.

"Tell me!" I demanded again.

"Okay, fine." She turned to face me directly. "I think the last movie I saw was *The Lion King*."

I stifled a chuckle.

"I mean, whatever, I love to binge throwbacks too. No shame in that. Live action or animated?"

Jane pressed her lips into a firm line, like she was holding something back. "The, uh, cartoon one," she admitted, pausing for a moment. "To be honest, I didn't even know they'd made a newer one."

This time, I couldn't hold back my laughter.

"But how?! It came out years ago! It streams on the same service!"

"You said you wouldn't make fun of me, Kate! Not cool," Jane whined, even though she grinned ear-to-ear.

She can laugh at herself. I like that.

"When did the original Lion King even come out?" I asked. I grabbed my cell phone from the table to do a quick search. Jane filled the silence as I typed.

"See, I told you you'd have to pick!" She covered her face with her hands.

My search results popped up on my phone. 1994.

I reminded myself to gauge her interests before starting a list of recs. The girl needed a serious movie update.

"Well, you might be onto something anyway," I said. "Let's do our paper on *The Lion King*. It honestly kind of writes itself. Mufasa gives his life to save Simba from the stampeding wildebeests. If that isn't selfless, I don't know what is."

Jane laughed, and we dug right into the paper. Our voices echoed through the large space as we swapped ideas. Getting along with Jane was easy. She was really smart but also down to earth. It was too bad she kept to herself in the back of Mrs. Marsh's class. I was sure if the other kids got to know her, they would discover how sweet she was.

When we'd completed our final sentence, I flipped the paper back over to the front and wrote my name in the top right corner.

I paused and slapped my forehead with my palm.

"I feel so stupid asking this. But what is your last name?"

"Oh, don't worry about it. It's Wright, but don't put my name down on the paper. You basically wrote the whole thing yourself. I might as well write my own later. This was fun though. I liked having someone to hang out with." Jane beamed, and her smile made her cool blue eyes sparkle brighter.

"I had a lot of fun too," I replied. "But I feel really bad. You honestly want me to claim all the credit for this?"

"C'mon, Kate, I barely contributed anything. I'll think of something else. A book or something. It's no big deal."

"If you say so," I said, gathering up my pencil and paper, then stuffing them into a binder in my backpack. "I think I'd better get home. My mom will be calling soon to check on me from work. Do you want to walk home together?"

"No, not tonight," Jane said, blushing. "I've got more chem studying to do here. But I'll see you tomorrow!"

"Okay," I said, noticing how the colors of the stained-glass windows had grown richer as the time had passed. "But don't stay too late. This place might be kinda creepy when it's dark. Evil Uncle Scar could be lurking in the shadows. Then pop out and sing at you or something."

Jane let out a snort, before breaking into a deep, infectious belly laugh. "Yeah, good tip. I'll keep an eye out."

I headed for the back library doors that opened up to the school yard. I glanced over my shoulder one last time. Jane's shoulders were still moving up and down with laughter.

I let the door close behind me and headed for home.

Chapter Seven

Heat singed my fingers, face, and exposed knees through the rips of my jeans. Like a million invisible daggers stabbing my skin. My heart pounded as flames surrounded me. I was back in the same room as before—clearly a classroom, but I wasn't sure where. I choked on the thick, black smoke, burning my throat. Through the fog, I tried to make out more details. The flames devoured a book and notebook on the floor nearby. The inferno disintegrated colorful posters from the walls, stools on the floor, and decorations hanging from the ceiling. I remembered those. I'd narrowly avoided being hit by one of them last time I was trapped.

The fire marched toward me, ready to swallow me whole.

The door. Find the door, Kate.

I took off in a sprint.

I tried the handle on the wooden door, but again, it wouldn't turn. Had to be locked. I pounded on the door with my fists, wet with sweat and flying with adrenaline.

"PLEASE HELP ME! I'M BEGGING YOU, PLEASE!"

All of a sudden, I stopped, shocked by a horrifying realization.

I didn't know how I knew, but I was not alone. My senses warned that someone was outside that locked door. Why weren't they helping me?

Did they leave me here... on purpose?

* * *

I JOLTED AWAKE, GASPING FOR AIR, TEARS STREAMING DOWN my face. The desperation running through me was too real to be from a nightmare.

What in the heck is wrong with me?

I reached for my phone on my nightstand. The lock screen read 10:14 P.M. Mom's newscast was still on.

Phone in hand, I ran for the light switch next to my door and flipped it on with such force, I thought it might break. There'd be no surprises if anyone lurked in my room. I ran downstairs to the living room and switched on the TV. Mom smiled as she bantered with her brown-haired, chipper co-anchor about some happy farmer story. Her smile helped me finally catch my breath.

Chapter Eight

> Arrested by police for vandalism. Made a sandwich for you though before they booked me. It's in the fridge.

And sent. Mom had her morning text, so she'd know I'd arrived safely to Ravendale Middle for day three. My phone buzzed.

> Oh shoot. No bail money.

> P.S. Good thing you fed me. Forgot I have a meet-and-greet with the mayor this morning. Going from there to work. Love you, kiddo.

I shrugged. Maybe if Mom messed up badly enough, it wouldn't be too late to get our place back in Peoria.

A kid can dream.

The temperature felt comfortable when I walked into Mrs. Marsh's room. Maybe someone had finally called a repairman. I shuffled past other students to reach the back row. But today, it was just me—no gray sweater and no Jane at the desk to the left of mine. No chemistry book, no sign of her anywhere. I hoped she wasn't sick. I figured I could DM her on social media at lunch. I hadn't gotten around to following her yet. It seemed strange to think I'd already found someone in this school cool enough to want to DM about random stuff. I sat down and pulled out my paper to hand in at the end of class.

Mrs. Marsh spent the full hour lecturing about voice in writing. She stated that since *The Diary of the Young Girl* was made up of diary entries, the language told us who Anne was at the time. While character voice wasn't part of our assignment, she hoped some of us were brave enough to venture into that topic in our papers. I doodled in my notebook, confident that we missed the boat on that part, given our selection of an animated movie. It was okay. At least our punctuation was perfect.

Jane had said she would write her own paper, but I didn't feel right claiming all the credit for work we'd done together. I'd written Kate Sablowsky at the top right corner of the paper and Jane Wright directly beneath it.

The bell rang.

"Okay, class, that's our time," Mrs. Marsh sang out. "Please drop your paper on my desk on your way out. Make it a super day!"

A line formed as students stepped into the aisle one-by-one to drop off their papers. Many of them had opted to work in pairs, so I was glad I'd taken Jane up on her offer to write together. Being the only soul in the last row, I dropped off my essay last. It sat on top of the short stack that had formed. I headed toward the door.

"Kate?" Mrs. Marsh asked quietly, her sing-song nature suddenly gone. I looked back at her from the doorway. "Sweetheart, why don't you come back here a minute."

I returned to the front of the classroom to face her. She sat at her desk, her hands folded neatly before her. Concern wrinkled her brow.

"Kate, you're new, and you want the others to like you. That's a perfectly natural feeling, dear, but I don't find this little joke very funny."

Mrs. Marsh's face was completely serious. I didn't know that I had ever seen her without a smile plastered ear-to-ear. Her energy was off.

"What are you talking about, Mrs. Marsh? What joke?"

"Including Jane Wright's name on your paper," she said in a hushed tone. She glanced toward the hallway.

"We worked on this together—" I began, but Mrs. Marsh cut me off.

"I want to reiterate, Kate, you are a bright girl, but these kinds of ruses won't get you very far." Mrs. Marsh's normally warm, brown eyes seemed to be pleading with me to explain myself, but I had no idea what she wanted me to say. My temple pounded, the beginning of a headache coming on.

What did I do wrong?

"Mrs. Marsh, with all due respect, I have no idea what you are talking about." My voice rose slightly as I defended myself.

"Kate, it's impossible for Jane to have helped you with your assignment, and I think you know that. Really, dear, it's time to put an end to this joke."

The edges of my vision blurred, causing the image of Mrs. Marsh to flicker. There had to have been some kind of terrible misunderstanding.

Did something happen to my friend?

At least, I thought she was my friend.

"Okay, I mean, I know Jane wasn't in class today, but—"

"Because Jane Wright died many years ago," Mrs. Marsh whispered, clearly irritated. Her voice caught with emotion, but she continued. "It was an extremely difficult time for the school and all of Ravendale. The fire changed some people here forever. It isn't funny to write her name on your paper for attention."

Then, the entire room shook. All of the blood rushed from my head, making the headache worse. I couldn't catch a deep enough breath to steady myself. And the chill that had been missing in the classroom burst back.

"There's got to be some mistake, Mrs. Marsh," I said through chattering teeth. "I don't know why you're acting like Jane isn't a student here."

"Sweetheart, she died before I ever *started* at Ravendale Middle School."

This had to be another one of my crazy nightmares. It just couldn't possibly be true.

How could Jane be dead? *And to have died* years *ago?*

We'd just hung out yesterday.

I realized I was still standing in front of Mrs. Marsh's desk. She gazed at me, expecting an apology—or, really, any kind of response from me whatsoever. I didn't have the strength to try to explain to her that Jane was in her class every day, just like me. The only thing I could do was run.

Chapter Nine

I slammed our front door shut and let my body collapse against it. My back struck the door so hard, Mom's "Home Sweet Home" sign shook on the other side.

My legs laid still for the first time since running from Mrs. Marsh's classroom all the way home. I gasped for air. Sweat dripped down my face, and my T-shirt stuck to my back.

I fired off a text to Bailey. Alone and scared, I had to say something to someone.

> GET ME OUT OF HERE, BAILS

But I hadn't thought it through. When she responded, asking what was wrong, I knew I couldn't explain my situation. She would think I was having a breakdown from the move. I played it safe in my response. As well as anyone could anyway, when they couldn't think straight.

> Just homework lol

But nothing about what had played out at school was funny. The spinning in my head wouldn't stop even at home. Still, I quickly made my way to the living room. Mom kept her tablet in the top drawer of the end table next to the couch. I wobbled my way over and yanked open the drawer. I punched in her passcode and sent an email from her account to my school.

Front Office Staff,

I am sorry I didn't personally stop in to check Kate out from class, but she called me to pick her up. She seems to have caught some kind of stomach bug and will be out the rest of the day.

Thanks,

Maria Silver

The little "sent" whoosh sounded, and I relaxed onto the couch. I finally managed my deepest inhale yet since my encounter with Mrs. Marsh. I swiped out of Mom's email account and opened the internet browser. I typed "Jane Wright Ravendale, Iowa" into the search bar. My breath quickened again when I lowered my pointer finger to press search. An answer I didn't and couldn't believe might be on the other side of that click. Then again, I still clung to the hope that this was just a really long nightmare.

"There has to be some explanation for this," I whispered out loud, my heart pounding in my chest.

CLICK.

The first hit that popped up was a newspaper article from *The Ravendale Times* with a headline that, again, made everything spin.

Questions remain 20 years after deadly middle school fire

I slowly brought my shaking hand to the article and selected it. It couldn't be true until I saw her face.

CLICK.

A neat, brown bob. A pale and perfect complexion. A gray sweater buttoned all the way to the neck with a crisp, white collar popping out the top. Jane's photo was positioned next to a grainy, aged photo of Ravendale Middle School, blackened, burnt, and parts of it reduced to rubble. I recognized the damaged part of the building as the current science wing. The walls were gone and anything that used to be inside was dissolved into unrecognizable soot.

My insides twisted.

I brought my eyes back to Jane's smiling face. The photo was a posed shot, probably for the yearbook. She looked exactly as I knew her, but the photo quality was poor, as though it had been taken with a very old camera. That brought me to the year of the article. 2015.

If 2015 marked twenty years since the fire, that meant Jane died in 1995. Before I was even born.

It was all too much to handle. My brain whirled, sending the letters twisting and turning and making them hard to read.

The article explained that a fire had erupted in Ravendale Middle School on October 10, 1995, around 5:45 P.M. Firefighters identified it as a structural fire, originating in the school's chemistry lab. Police reported at the time that there was only one person in the building when the fire broke out, and that person was seventh-grader Jane Wright. She perished in the blaze.

The Wright family declined to be interviewed for the anniversary story. However, they told police after the initial fire that Jane had left them a note on the morning of October 10 saying she planned to grab a snack at the diner and work on homework after school. She would be home late. Jane was an only child. No one at the diner reported seeing her, and her parents had no idea why she had been at the school. No one at the school, staff or classmates, had any knowledge of what she was doing either.

I realized this was before the time of cell phones; no way to check in with a text.

I felt heartbroken, and I'd only just met Jane.

Well, could I even call it that?

We couldn't have met because she couldn't be real. My stomach churned, picturing her poor mother and father with no real answers about what led to their daughter's death.

I'd never believed in the concept of closure. I probably didn't have real "closure" from the fact my dad left Mom and me, but I'd learned to find peace with it. I doubted the Wrights had been able to find that peace.

BUZZZZ.

My cell phone vibrated with an incoming text. My hands still shook, and I struggled to fish my phone out of my pocket. The case slid around on my sweaty palm.

Jane can't reach me on a cell phone, right? The thought terrified me. *What is she?*

> You get one chance to truthfully tell me why I just got a response from your school about picking you up early.

Oh, man. Mom!
I quickly typed:

> I have the chills and feel like I'm going to be sick. Didn't want to interrupt your meeting. Walked home. I'm sorry, I should've told you.

I pressed send. Mom quickly responded that she would let it

slide this one time, but I had to check my temperature and let her know if I had a fever. I swore I didn't.

The only place that seemed safe was under my heavy comforter on my bed. I switched on the lamp on my nightstand and burrowed under my covers, my eyes peeking out the top. I was not going to turn that light off.

A thought punched me in my already-queasy stomach: *Am I like Bubbe after all? Do I have her "gift?"*

If so, where was the gift receipt? I didn't want to be like her. I slapped at the charm dangling from my wrist.

I blinked and looked around my room, trying to calm myself down. I tried to avoid having my gaze land on the photo that sat on my desk in a banged-up, wooden frame. An old photo of Mom, Bubbe, and me at a picnic. I smiled in between them like a loser, without my two front teeth. I focused instead on my lamp, the light over my bed, the movies on my shelf. But my eyes betrayed me and took me there. I saw my bubbe, smiling from behind her giant, brown-framed glasses.

Life's not just the here and now.

Tears welled in my eyes. I'd misunderstood Bubbe's saying all this time. She was trying to prepare me. In case I was like her. In case I ever saw people like Jane.

It finally sunk in that this wasn't a nightmare. Whatever was happening was real.

I'd have to face the truth. A tear spilled out of one eye and rolled down my cheek. I might even have to face Jane tomorrow.

Chapter Ten

It was the first serious "I've arrived safely to school" text I'd sent my mom in at least a year:

> Here but still not feeling great. Might call you in a bit.

My message was true though. I couldn't bring myself to tell her about Jane and what I had experienced at school. I loved Mom like a best friend, and I could always confide in her. But I wasn't ready for this. What if she confirmed I had Bubbe's gift after all? What then?

Clearly, it had skipped Mom's generation, which seemed like more of a gift than the "gift" itself. As terrifying as my situation was, I had to find Jane—or whatever she was—and get answers on my own.

My phone buzzed.

> I feel like even your text has a fever. You don't sound like you. Call me if you need me.

I hoped Mom could sense my eyes rolling from home.

So dramatic.

The temperature was slightly cooler that morning. I'd worn a zip-up hoodie for my walk to school but underestimated how much I'd sweat from nerves.

I waited a few extra beats before heading toward Mrs. Marsh's room after the first bell. I had no clue how I'd keep my cool if I saw Jane. I also dreaded Mrs. Marsh trying to pick up our conversation where we'd left off. I watched my classmates, one-by-one, shuffle into class. When the hallway emptied, I gritted my teeth and almost jogged in. Throwing myself into the situation felt like ripping off a Band-Aid.

My eyes were focused on the speckled tan floor tiles. I needed a minute to adjust before I looked up and saw her face. The same face from the yearbook photo, frozen in time.

By the time I reached the second row, I took a deep breath and shot my head upwards, scanning the back of the classroom. No gray sweater. No brown bob. My eyes searched and searched, but Jane wasn't there. My chest fell with a sigh of relief.

I realized I'd been so focused on seeing Jane that I hadn't noticed the absence of the chill in the classroom. It was then I put the two things together. The chill wasn't an air-conditioning problem. Sort of like when a ghost was about to appear in *The Sixth Sense*. It was her.

I dropped my backpack next to my desk and sat as quickly as I could, glancing over my shoulder. I didn't know if I expected the bogeyman to be behind me, but it was hard to feel safe.

Mrs. Marsh stood before the class with her arms folded. Her mop of brown and gray curls was gathered on top of her head with a big claw clip, heart-shaped dangle earrings swaying. Her eyes were fixed on me, a look of concern on her furrowed brow.

Mrs. Marsh's look seemed to say she wasn't angry about yesterday. That everything was okay, and if I needed her, she would be there. A wave of gratitude rushed over me. Mrs. Marsh wasn't just doing her job—she seemed to care.

Given how I felt, I couldn't pay attention to Mrs. Marsh's lecture. We had moved on from *The Diary of a Young Girl* to another novel, but I hadn't done the assigned reading. I sat quietly and pretended to be paying attention. My eyes took every opportunity when Mrs. Marsh glanced away to search the room for Jane.

How does this work exactly? Does she walk through walls? Will she appear out of thin air like Harry Potter with his invisibility cloak?

I'd almost grown used to everything shaking by then. The back of my sleeve doubled as a rag to wipe the sweat from the sides of my face. About halfway through class, I couldn't take it anymore. My hand shot into the air like a missile.

"Mrs. Marsh?" I called out. "May I go to the restroom, please?"

"Of course, dear," she replied with that same look of concern.

I kept my eyes cast downward, choosing to focus again on the floor tiles. I left my things where they were and booked it out of there. I took the sharp right turn out of the classroom, down the empty hallway. My quick steps kept a steadier beat than my choppy, uneven breaths. If I didn't look up, maybe she wouldn't appear? I'd been so ready to face her but realized, in that moment, the entire scenario was just too much.

I ducked through the door into the girls' restroom and beelined for the middle sink. I grabbed hold of both sides of it with my hands and squeezed, stabilizing myself with its sturdiness. I looked at myself in the mirror and took a few deep breaths, in and out. In and out.

Just then, the hair on my arms prickled. My spine tingled. The chill returned. I gripped the sink tighter and forced myself to continue with my breathing. In and—

"How was Mary Poppins today?" a familiar-but-shy voice whispered from the corner, sending me an inch into the air.

I swiveled around as quickly as I could, even though I already knew who I was about to see. Dressed the way she always had been, holding her chemistry book in her hand. I had been trying so hard to avoid Jane that I shocked myself, facing her. She took one step forward, then stopped. She glanced at the floor. In fact, every part of her expression was turned downward in a sad way. I wondered if she was worried about scaring me off. Maybe it was shame. Something kept me from running. She couldn't be there to hurt me.

"She was nice enough," I began, quietly. "After everything that happened yesterday anyway." My voice trailed off.

Jane avoided meeting my eyes. She owed me answers. I waited.

"I overheard the conversation," she said.

My eyes scanned the bottom of the bathroom stalls to be sure we were alone.

I got the impression Jane wasn't used to interacting with people like me. That is, people with a pulse. That was weird to think. It was time to cut to the chase.

"I need to know what you are. I just don't understand," I said, feeling braver in the moment. I couldn't believe I was about to say the word out loud. "Are you a *ghost*?"

Jane finally met my gaze. Her cool, blue eyes begged me to hear her out. My question hung in the air for a moment.

"You could say that," she murmured. Her eyes welled before a single tear fell down the side of her face.

"You died in 1995. Here. Why didn't you tell me?" My fists clenched with frustration, but at the same time, I felt a pull in my chest. My heart ached to see someone that sweet in pain, alive or not.

"And say what? 'Hi, welcome to Ravendale. I'm Jane. I'm

dead,'" she mocked. "I have tried and tried over the years to talk to people. To make people see me. It's never worked."

Jane threw her arms up in exasperation, the pages of her chemistry book slapping against the covers.

"I don't know what made me try to talk to you, but the day you started at Ravendale, I got a feeling that you might be different," Jane continued. "That maybe you could help me. I'm stuck here. I can't... pass on."

She took two steps forward.

I didn't want to explain to her that she was right. I *was* different, thanks to Bubbe's stupid gift. I skipped past that.

"Help you?" I questioned.

"I pretended to be a student to meet you." Jane dabbed at her eyes with the back of her pale hand. "When you answered me, I couldn't believe it. I had to think fast. I imagined you'd figure everything out about me eventually. I didn't know when, and I knew I couldn't be the one to tell you. You'd have to overcome the shock yourself. I'd be here whenever you were ready."

She was right. If she had told me she was dead, I would have either laughed at her or run for the hills.

"And yes, I need your help," Jane continued. A moment of silence made her plea all the more terrifying before she resumed. "I don't know why I died."

How is that possible?

I couldn't process what she was saying. I shook my head to make the room stop spinning.

"I read a newspaper article online," I said. "You left a note for your parents that you were going to go to the diner after school, but you never showed up. You died in a fire in the chem lab."

I couldn't believe I was explaining to Jane how she lost her life.

"I know that," she said. "I remember the fire. I just can't

remember why it happened. How it happened. How I wound up there."

She hesitated and closed her mouth, holding something back. There was more.

"I don't understand," I mumbled, my insides clenching, fearing what she would say next. "How am I supposed to help you figure that out?"

"I need you to... I don't know, investigate," she said, her cool eyes staring into mine.

The spinning got worse. My mind screamed.

"You're asking me to talk to people who were alive at the time? To learn why you were really at the school?"

I peered at the restroom door, afraid someone might walk in on this unbelievable conversation.

"Yes, but that's not all. Kate, I think someone may have killed me."

Chapter Eleven

L eaving school that day, my conversation with Jane played on a loop in my head.

"I can't explain it," she'd said. "The fire was burning, and I banged on a door for help. Kate, I had a feeling someone knew I was inside and didn't come to save me."

What a horrible secret to be holding onto for more than twenty years. I couldn't believe it had been so long and investigators (real investigators) had never gotten to the bottom of what happened. Jane was just a kid.

One thing was for certain though. I knew the source of the nightmares I'd been having since coming to Ravendale. The ones where I was trapped in a burning room. Jane and I had apparently formed some kind of deep connection. The terror I felt in my sleep was what Jane experienced that October night. Knowing that made me feel sick all over again. It was somehow my job to help free her of that pain and move on.

"There are rules for people like me," Jane had explained. "You kind of just immediately understand them... when *it* happens. It's like a dark, unclear rule book is planted in your brain. The rules are awful, and it took me a long time to accept them. Because I don't have answers about what happened, I'm stuck here where I died. People who understand their deaths and are at peace with them have choices. They can pass on or continue to explore this world until they're *ready* to pass on. But while they're still here, they're alone."

"Alone?" That felt like a gut punch. "Why would anyone choose to be alone? Don't you at least have each other? Other—well, you know."

Nice, Kate.

Saying "ghosts" felt taboo, even if it wasn't.

"We can *feel* others like us," Jane had said. "Living people with gifts, like yours, supposedly feel a chill or shiver when people like me come around."

I nodded, confirming this.

"Well, we feel that, too, but we can't see or hear each other. There have been others I've felt around the school over the years. No clue who they are though. None of them have wound up stuck here long-term, like me."

It seemed like a miserable way to live. Or not live.

Gosh, this is confusing.

Jane opened her mouth to speak again. Her expression was as serious as I'd seen it, and her voice lowered.

"That's why I think I was *murdered*."

The last word sent a fresh chill through my entire body. I wrapped my arms around my waist as I shivered. Partially for warmth, partially to keep from throwing up. I didn't know the right words to say, but I suddenly had a better understanding of my assignment.

Jane needed answers, and so did I. Someone had gotten away with murder in Ravendale, Iowa. That someone could still be out there, preparing to hurt somebody else. Maybe he or she already had. I had never considered myself the heroic type, but I couldn't bear the thought of Jane being stuck at school, alone for all eternity. Or another family going through the same hurt the Wrights had been through.

Jane was as confused as I was on where to begin our investigation, if we could even call it that. It was my idea to start with Mom's TV station. After school, I walked to our house. I figured my plan would work best if I made my move closer to news time.

KTRD was about a five- to ten-minute drive from home, I'd heard Mom say. Of course, I'd have to make the trip on foot. When the time came, I punched the address into my maps app and set out, grateful the temperature had warmed during the day. I plodded along, one foot in front of the other, down Main Street's sidewalk.

The TV station's tower loomed above the trees, still lush with green leaves. As I got closer, I could see the building was made of orange and tan bricks. It kind of looked like a fire house, if not for the giant lighted sign spelling out the station's call letters. The building was nothing spectacular to look at, but it could hold a treasure trove of answers for Jane and me.

I walked through the first set of glass doors at the front of the building, then gave a tug on the second set immediately inside. Those were locked. I was relieved to know a crazy TV fan or angry story subject couldn't barge into the building where my mom worked. I pushed the small, beige button to the left of the doors and heard a beeping sound.

"May I help you?" a nasally voice responded.

"Hi. I'm Kate Sablowsky, Maria Silver's daughter. Just here to surprise her." I forced a smile to sound as innocent as possible.

"Sure, come on in," the voice answered.

Within seconds, I learned the nasally-sounding woman was a secretary named Gwen. She looked a few years older than Mom with red-framed glasses perched on the edge of her nose and a collection of thin braids tied back in a neat ponytail. Her long red fingernails tapped away on her computer.

It almost hurt to admit to myself that she was the first person of color I'd seen since moving to Ravendale. Being Jewish meant others in town might view me as different. It's no secret small midwestern towns don't have large Jewish populations. I'd experienced my share of weird looks over the years in places bigger than Ravendale: at school when I told teachers I'd miss class over the high holidays, at a big-box store when Mom asked why they didn't carry Hanukkah candles, in the cafeteria when my sandwich had matzah instead of bread during Passover. Not that Jews and Black people were rare specimens, but there was peace in knowing someone else in this town was different too. It sucked that I had to lie to her face.

"You know what, Ms. Gwen?" I said, my cheeks flushing with my deceit. "Now that I think of it, Mom is probably rushing to get ready for her 5 P.M. newscast. I can keep myself busy for a while before I surprise her."

"Sure, hun, whatever you'd like. You're welcome to wait here." She gestured with her long nails to a brown chair.

I swallowed and decided to try my luck.

"Actually, if it's not too much trouble, would you mind showing me the station's tape archive? I love the old-school stuff, the old tape decks. It'd be kind of neat to browse my new home's history, you know?" I raised my eyebrows.

Gwen looked back at me. I could tell she was smart. She'd probably see right through my little ruse, skip paging Mom altogether, and go straight to calling security.

"You know, we aren't supposed to let visitors back there unsupervised."

I sat in silence and stared back at her with the biggest, most-innocent eyes I could muster.

The subtle lines in Gwen's forehead relaxed a bit.

"Okay, I can tell this isn't your first time," she said. "Maria's worked all over. I'll show you where the tapes are, but if anything gets damaged, I'm going to tell your mom you snuck back there. We clear?"

She pushed her frames back up her nose where they belonged. I knew I liked her.

"Crystal," I said.

We went through a door to the left of her desk and then down a long hallway with fluorescent lighting. We eventually turned left again and walked into a room lined with small boxed videotapes that fit into older news camera models. The air smelled dusty. The room obviously wasn't regularly used or cleaned.

Gwen gestured toward a musty desk in the corner. It held an old-school TV monitor attached to a tape deck with a large circular knob to rewind and fast forward. Probably a lot of young journalists wouldn't know what to do with this type of retro machinery, but I was a pro. Back when Mom was a reporter just starting out in the business, she didn't always have someone to babysit me. She would sometimes bring me to work for a couple hours after daycare and let me play with the old knobs and tapes at her station. I would watch old news clips of men and women with funny haircuts and loud blazers, reporting from county fairs and stuff. I only ever pulled the film out of a video tape once when it wasn't playing correctly. I lost TV privileges for two weeks. Never made that mistake again.

"Remember how to get back to my desk from here?" Gwen asked me.

"I sure do, Ms. Gwen. Thanks again. I'll be back up front soon."

With a swift nod, Gwen closed the door behind her. Her heels clicked back down the hallway.

I didn't have a lot of time.

The fire that killed Jane happened in 1995. I took off like the

Tasmanian devil in *Space Jam*, searching the tape boxes for dates. Very few news stories were archived that way anymore. It was only the old stuff. 2000... 1999... 1998... I was getting closer. When I hit 1995, my pace and breathing quickened.

"October, October, October, where are you?" I whispered under my breath.

Then, I saw it.

The worn sticker label on the side of the box read "DEADLY RAVENDALE MIDDLE SCHOOL FIRE." I grabbed the case, knocking down a few of the tapes next to it with my impatience. I quickly put them back where they belonged, so as to not get Gwen in trouble.

With the tape I needed now firmly in my hands, I scurried back to the desk with the monitor, opened the case, and popped it in the deck. The familiar WHIRRRRR sound of the tape pierced the silence, and an eternity seemed to pass before the video came across the screen.

Then, up popped an image of a female reporter with big '90s hair and a bright blue blouse reporting after dark. The little clock in the corner of the screen showed it was 10 P.M. Bright lights lit up her face as she held one of those vintage mic flags with the station's logo on it. What she stood in front of took my breath away. The camera panned away from her to show Ravendale Middle School's charred remains, the air still hazy from smoke. I again recognized the damaged area as the wing that housed the chem lab. The reporter addressed the worst part of the tragedy.

At this time, the cause of the fire remains unknown. The state fire marshal is on the way to the scene to investigate. Multiple sources tell us it's likely the human remains inside were those of a student. Witnesses say a student's parents arrived here earlier this evening, distraught, and said their daughter was missing. Police aren't confirming that at this hour, but if that is the case,

*it's unclear what she would have been doing inside at the time
the blaze broke out.*

The video cut to a group of onlookers gathered together
outside the police tape. The shot only lasted a few seconds, but I
still managed to see two familiar figures in the crowd. I punched
the pause button. First, there was a woman I recognized as an
eighth-grade teacher. I pulled up the school's website on my
phone and scrolled through the faculty page until I landed on the
right face.

Mrs. Nettles, French.

Turning back to the video, I didn't need to look up the man
standing next to her. It was Mr. Davis. It figured he'd been a
teacher there for many years, based on his general lack of enthusi-
asm. His hair was brown and full then, and the frames on his
glasses were thinner. He didn't have the same wrinkles across his
forehead. Mrs. Nettles held a baby up to her shoulder with a
blanket wrapped around its little body. Even from a distance, I
could tell her eyes were swollen from crying. Mr. Davis appeared
serious but reflective. He wasn't the emotional type, but still, I
imagined he was sad too.

I rewound the news report a few more times and watched it
in full. I wanted to be sure I wasn't missing anything. The report
aired only hours after the fire happened. Authorities hadn't even
confirmed yet that it was Jane who died. Still, knowing which
teachers were at the school at the time gave me some direction.

I knew my time was running short, and Gwen could pop back
in to check on me at any moment. I punched the eject button and
threw the tape back in its plastic case before returning it to its
dusty spot on the shelf.

With one final look around the room to be sure I hadn't left
anything out of place, I switched off the light, stepped into the
hallway, and shut the door.

By the time I made it back to Gwen's desk, I'd fired off a text to Mom. There were only a couple minutes left of the 5 p.m. newscast. I sat down in one of the lobby chairs.

> Feeling better so went for a walk. Up for a random, bored visitor? Come to the lobby!

A few minutes later, Mom breezed in from the same hall I'd just walked through. She wore a bright pink wraparound dress and a serious expression that took me by surprise.

"Hey, kiddo! Happy to see you, but why the heck did you walk down here by yourself? This isn't home or school." She was scolding me, I figured, but she wasn't very convincing. Her arms were stretched out, and she enveloped me into a bear hug.

"Sorry, Mom. Just wanted to explore," I fibbed. "Won't make a habit out of it."

From the confines of Mom's embrace, I made eye contact with Gwen behind her computer screen. I shot her a quick grimace that said I knew I was in trouble. I didn't need to say anything else. She already knew the tape archive situation was our little secret.

Mom continued to hug me close. It all felt a little mushy to me, but knowing what Jane went through had me missing my mom more than normal. What if something ever happened to me, and she was just... *alone*? I shuddered.

"Kate, are you still sick? It's like you have the chills or something." Mom pulled back from the hug to get a good look at me. She did that mom thing where she checked my forehead with her hand.

Does that trick even work?

I pushed her arm aside.

"Mom, quit worrying. I'm fine," I said with a dramatic eye roll, although my tone didn't match it.

"Well, since you're already out, stop and pick up some soup

from the Chinese restaurant down the block just in case. It's on your way home." She handed me twenty dollars. "And text me the minute you make it back."

"Got it," I said.

Mom really was the best. I gulped, sick that I was about to lie to her face. There was a lot of that happening in KTRD's lobby that day.

"Oh, and I am going to go to school a little early tomorrow. I want to meet with Mrs. Marsh about my first writing assignment. Make sure I'm meeting her standards, you know?"

"*Meeting* her standards? Kiddo, you *are* the standard!" Mom planted a kiss on top of my head and turned to head back down the hall. "Love you!"

I really loved her too.

It made me all the more nervous for what I had to do the next morning.

Chapter Twelve

Flames towered above me, chewing away at the ceiling overhead. Knowing what I did about Jane, it was obvious I was in the Ravendale Middle School chem lab. A thick veil of smoke hung in the air, making it nearly impossible to see. Panic set in, but I'd been there before. I knew the space. I tried to take in what I could. Between clouds of darkness, I saw the lab station tables and stools. The engulfed ceiling decorations appeared to be models of atoms.

My observations were cut short as I choked on the smoke. The heat was unbearable. I knew I needed to escape and forced my body to move. I ran for the door and grabbed the warm handle. I already knew it would be locked. I took a shallow breath and screamed.

"Please help! Let me out!" I shouted, throwing my body into the door.

"No one's coming, Kate," said a hushed voice. "It's just us in here."

I spun around and barely made out the shape of Jane. She had ash and soot on her pale face.

"*NO, JANE! We can get out of here! We need to get out of here!*" I shouted at her, turning back to the door to continue my frantic pounding.

I brought my face to the narrow window in the door that looked out to the hallway. Even if I was able to shatter the glass, my arm wouldn't be long enough to reach the handle on the other side of the door. But maybe, just maybe, I could see someone out there to help.

Mrs. Nettles stepped into view. She cradled a baby, wrapped in a blanket, like in that archive video. She acted as if she couldn't hear my screams and walked away.

My legs trembled in defeat. I turned to Jane, but she was already gone.

* * *

I LURCHED UPWARD IN MY BED, GASPING FOR AIR. SWEAT had soaked through my pajamas. I sat there in stillness; my chest was the only part of me that moved as I struggled to breathe. I wiped my brow with the back of my arm. This was the worst nightmare I'd had yet.

Could Mrs. Nettles be responsible for Jane's death? I hadn't met her in my first few days at Ravendale Middle, but the images I'd seen didn't make her seem like a monster.

I tapped my cell phone and saw it was only 2:32 A.M. Thank goodness. After my nightmare, I felt I needed to approach the situation at school more gently than I had planned. The truth was, I didn't know Mrs. Nettles or what she was capable of at all.

Chapter Thirteen

The alarm on my phone started chirping a happy tune about an hour before it normally sounded. But it wasn't a normal day. The alarm taunted me, knowing what I had to do. I rolled over and switched it off before the noise disturbed Mom.

I lay in bed for a few minutes, scrolling stupid videos on social media and taking deep breaths. I needed to keep my cool. I also needed to debrief my friend, who just so happened to be a freaking ghost, about my progress.

I grabbed a blue T-shirt, gray hoodie, and jeans, then headed to the bathroom for a shower. A quick ponytail and some Pop-Tarts, and I was out the door.

It was another nice day, off to a cool start before the afternoon heat rolled in. I wondered how long it would be until autumn arrived and the leaves started falling. Then again, that's just what I needed—leafless trees to make this town feel even spookier.

Don't be dramatic, Kate.

As I crossed the street to school, I pulled my phone from my pocket and texted Mom.

> Followed a trail of candy to an old witch's house. Love you.

As usual, my phone buzzed a couple seconds later.

> YUM! Bring me some!

I stuck my phone back in my pocket and yanked open the school's main entrance door. I didn't know if it would be unlocked at 7 A.M., but it was. All the lights were on inside. I started my trek down the main hallway and turned right toward the stairwell that would carry me up to the third floor, where the foreign language classrooms were located.

When I reached the third floor, I kept my steps light. I didn't know where to find Mrs. Nettles, and I didn't want anyone to see me. Everyone knew seventh graders didn't belong up there.

I recognized a poster of the blue, white, and red French flag outside room 306. The door stood open. I paused and closed my eyes. I took a deep breath and rehearsed the story I'd made up in my head to be sure I was ready. I knocked twice on the open wooden door to make my presence known before crossing the threshold.

A stout woman with tight brown curls and a fuzzy striped sweater pored over a stack of papers at her desk. She glanced up at me as I entered.

"Hi, come on in," Mrs. Nettles said with a smile, her eyes sparkling behind her black-framed glasses. Not a touch of makeup, which I respected. She finished marking the paper in front of her for another second while she waited for me to introduce myself. She then removed her glasses and set them aside.

I made my way to a desk across from hers and sat.

"Mrs. Nettles, I'm Kate Sablowsky," I began. "I'm not

enrolled in any foreign language classes yet, but I wanted to introduce myself."

"Yes, I've heard about you," she said, warmth reflected in her eyes. "Maria Silver's daughter! Pretty neat to live with a TV star, huh?"

Mrs. Nettles grinned and sat back in her chair. She appeared excited but still more subdued than Mrs. Marsh had been.

"Something like that," I said with a forced chuckle. "She loves French. She studied it in high school."

"Ah, *magnifique!*" she crooned.

I was trying to butter her up. Her smile suggested my plan was working. Still, I couldn't wait forever.

"Mrs. Nettles, this may seem kind of random, but I'm interested in filmmaking," I said. "I've noticed Ravendale Middle doesn't have a film club, and I want to change that."

I hoped the acting skills I'd perfected in my second-grade holiday pageant shined through.

"Well, the apple doesn't fall far from the tree!" she replied with a satisfied grin, folding her arms across her chest. "A love for the camera."

She seemed to believe me so far.

"I'm actually thinking about working on a project about safety improvements at Ravendale Middle since the fire that happened in 1995," I said.

I paused.

Mrs. Nettles's smile faltered at my last few words. She probably guessed what was coming next.

"I know you were a teacher here back then. I'm wondering if I could ask you a few questions."

I pulled a small, rectangular GoPro camera out of my backpack. Mom had gotten it for me for Hanukkah last year. I set it on the desk. To be respectful, I didn't press record. The gear was all for show anyway.

Mrs. Nettles looked at the camera with a nervous expression but didn't tell me to get out or anything.

"I don't know that I remember much about safety measures at the time, but I do remember that awful, awful day, Kate," she said. "I suppose Ravendale would have benefited from modern-day security cameras. Things we take for granted now. My understanding is no one knew why Jane was there that night."

"I'm not recording or anything yet," I reassured her. "I'm just curious what you remember from that day at school."

I'd watched my mom conduct a million of these interviews. It wasn't hard to keep the conversation going if you got a subject started.

"That's the thing," Mrs. Nettles said. "I was actually out on maternity leave that October. My little girl, Mary, was born on September second that year. Of course, I'd known Jane before then, but I'd been home for weeks before it happened."

Mrs. Nettles stopped and took a deep breath. The memory seemed to cause her pain.

"That must have been hard for you, to hear about it on the news or something like that," I said.

She nodded slowly, thoughtfully. "It really was. I first heard about the fire on the 6 o'clock news, and in a small town, word gets around so quickly. A friend called to tell me the Wrights had arrived at the school shortly thereafter, sobbing. Jane was a bright girl with her whole life ahead of her. A fantastic French student even as a seventh grader. She passed a proficiency exam and was in my class with all the eighth graders. As soon as I heard it was probably her, I bundled up Mary and we went down to the school together. I had to see everything with my own eyes."

Mrs. Nettles bit her lower lip. Her cheeks tinged red as she fought back tears. She couldn't have had anything to do with Jane's death. She had an obvious alibi, and she seemed to think very fondly of Jane. Plus, she had her hands full with a baby. I grabbed my GoPro and gently returned it to my bag.

"Mrs. Nettles," I said softly, "I really appreciate you taking the time to chat with me. When I get a focus for my project, I'll be sure to follow up. But before I go, I believe Mr. Davis was a teacher here back then too?"

I hoped she couldn't tell I was playing dumb.

"Yes. He was there that day," she confirmed. "If I remember correctly, he left that afternoon to go home and care for his mother. She was living with him at the time. That was a sad situation too. I'm afraid he enjoys talking about the fire as much as I do, which is not at all. I know he was horrified that the tragedy happened in his chem lab. He felt so terrible." She shook her head for emphasis.

Could Mr. Davis be the one we are after?

What motive did he have to harm one of his students? Like Mrs. Nettles, his involvement seemed far-fetched. But maybe he saw something peculiar that day. It was worth a shot.

I glanced at my cell phone. Too close to the first bell. I could see students approaching the building through the window. My talk with Mr. Davis would have to wait.

"Maybe I'll try to speak with him soon," I said with a polite smile. "Thanks again, Mrs. Nettles. It was nice to meet you."

"Anytime, *ma cherie*," she said with a sudden French accent. "I'm always here."

Unfortunately, so is Jane.

Poor Mrs. Nettles just didn't know that. She was a dead end, but Mr. Davis might be able to point me in the right direction.

Chapter Fourteen

A s I crossed back into the hallway, that now-familiar chill rippled down my spine. My shoulders shook. I knew Jane was there; I just didn't know where. The first-period bell would ring at any moment and the third-floor hallway was crawling with eighth graders.

Right before I entered the stairwell to make my way back to the first floor, I gave one last look down the hallway. And there she stood—before the window, past all the other students. She looked almost like an angel, as the morning sunlight shone around her silhouette. Her hands were by her side, her right hand clutched her chem book, and her eyes were fixed on me. She didn't say a word, but her gaze said she wanted to know what I'd learned since the last time we spoke.

I broke our eye contact, ducked my head, and proceeded down the stairs. Still, the chill lingered. It felt like Jane surrounded me. Like she was nowhere and everywhere at the same time.

I walked into Mrs. Marsh's classroom, hung my usual left, and walked to my back-row seat. Jane had beaten me there. She sat in her seat, too, her gray sweater and white collar looking exactly as they always had.

"What did you find out at the news station?" Jane whispered. She didn't wait for a response. "It sounds like Mrs. Nettles couldn't have been involved in the fire. I was listening in. Even all these years later, she seemed so sad. I think I remember liking her. I'm sure I did."

I stared straight ahead. I wasn't ignoring her, but now that I knew she was a ghost, I couldn't go around talking to her when other people could see. They'd think I was crazy.

"Kate, what's wrong? Are you mad at me?" Jane swiveled in her desk seat to face me.

I pulled a pen and notebook out of my backpack as Mrs. Marsh began the day's lesson. Today was all about tense: past, present, future. It struck me as ironic and sad that to Jane, tense would never matter. She was stuck in the past and present with no hope of a future—not without my help at least.

Can't talk in front of other people. Going to talk to Mr. Davis at lunch.

I scribbled the message on a blank piece of notebook paper. Jane read it and nodded.

The rest of the morning was a blur. Time seemed to drag on forever, but no matter what I tried, I couldn't concentrate. I also couldn't shake the chill that accompanied Jane throughout the school.

Here and there, I caught her staring at me, her pale skin glowing. The sight of her wasn't scary though. Her presence was a reminder I had a lot of digging to do.

The lunch hour couldn't come quickly enough. I dropped off my stuff in my locker, a few yards from Mr. Davis's classroom door. I clutched my GoPro to keep up the appearance of working on a film project. I took a few deep breaths and set off in a purposeful walk, leaving my nerves in the hall.

I poked my head in the doorway. Each stool sat perfectly in place. Mr. Davis leaned over a table, wiping it down with a rag. He peeked at me over his gold-framed glasses for a moment when I entered, but his cleanup activities didn't stop. His cream-colored polo shirt was tucked neatly into his khaki pants and buttoned all the way up. As always, he appeared very put-together. He didn't say a word. He was probably hoping I'd just buzz off.

"Ahem," I coughed. It was a corny introduction, but I'm not good at striking up chats with people. Somehow, Mom's genes failed me there. "Mr. Davis? I was hoping I could pick your brain about something."

His eyes met mine, then dropped down to the camera I was holding. He didn't say anything.

For sure, not a people person.

He continued to look at me, so I took that as my green light to go on.

"I'm hoping to start a student film club here," I said, mustering as much confidence as I could. "I learned Ravendale Middle doesn't have one. I wondered if you could help me with my first project."

"I don't do cameras," he said, his tone serious. He had finally stopped wiping the table.

"It's okay," I responded. "I'm not recording or anything. I just want to pick your brain. My project is about safety improvements here at the school. Since that big fire back in 1995."

I watched his face closely to gauge his reaction. Mr. Davis kept still, occasionally glancing down at my camera in an untrusting way.

"I don't know what I can add," he said. "I'm sure you know the fire broke out in my chem lab."

He didn't seem to want to volunteer any more information than what was asked.

"Yeah, I've heard that," I said, trying to keep my voice light. "Any idea how it started?"

I knew I sounded naïve. My questions were uncomfortable. No one liked to be pressed for details about something horrible.

His expression hadn't changed.

"They say it had to do with a burner. It was a tragedy, certainly, but my room was secure when I left it that day. I do now what I did then. I always lock up."

"So, you have no idea what that girl... Jane, right? What she was doing in your chem lab that evening?"

Mr. Davis walked toward his desk in the front right corner of the room. He sat in his chair. He didn't gesture for me to sit, but I did anyway. I pulled out the nearest stool and sat to face him.

"I don't know what I can say," he said, adjusting his glasses.

He appeared fidgety under the spotlight, but I couldn't blame him for that.

"I told the police everything the night it happened," he continued. "Jane was a student of mine. She was a bright girl. I don't know why she was in the lab or how any burner would have turned on. It was off when I left school that day."

"Do you remember about what time that was?" I asked, leaning slightly toward him, the way I'd seen Mom do a million times.

"I'm not sure what that has to do with a story about security upgrades," Mr. Davis said, a bit of a bite creeping into his tone. He continued, nonetheless. "I left at 4:30. My mother has since passed away, but at the time, she lived with me so I could take care of her. She had dementia and several other medical issues. I always left by 4:30, so I could have dinner ready for her around 5:30."

I picked up my GoPro. I didn't see a way Mr. Davis could

have been involved if he'd left more than an hour before the fire started and locked his room behind him. Plus, I could tell I was irritating him at that point.

"I'm, uh, sorry about your mom," I said softly. That part actually made me feel bad. Sure, he wasn't a friendly kind of guy, but he was caring for his mom after dealing with middle schoolers all day. "That's really all I can think to ask you."

"Alright," he said under his breath.

Mr. Davis didn't bother looking at me. I had rubbed him the wrong way. He stood up, opened his top left desk drawer and pulled out his lanyard containing an array of keys. He walked across the room and held the door handle, extending his arm as though he was inviting me into the hall. It was more like getting kicked out of his chem lab.

"If you'll excuse me, next period is when I usually eat my lunch," he said.

"Oh, s-s-sure," I stuttered, a bit embarrassed by the entire interaction. "Thanks, Mr. Davis. This will, uh, really help my project."

I started fidgeting with my GoPro, unsure of what else to do, and walked back to my locker.

Mr. Davis nodded, still avoiding eye contact, and closed his classroom door behind us. He seized a key on his lanyard, then turned the lock, methodically, as if he'd done it a thousand times before. He headed for the teacher's lounge.

Mr. Davis wasn't the type to even go to the restroom without locking his door behind him. He was careful. Sure, he was weird, but that didn't mean he was a murderer. Another name to cross off my list.

Jane stood at the far end of the seventh-grade hallway looking at me. Her eyebrows were raised in a hopeful way. I paused and looked back at her. A few students and faculty members roamed the hallway. It wasn't the right time to talk. I ever-so-slightly shook my head *no*. Her eyebrows fell in disappointment. I offered her a small, encouraging smile.

The truth was, I was in over my head. I had no idea what I was doing, and there were honestly many reasons to give up hope. I was scared to go to Mom, because I didn't know what having Bubbe's gift really meant. What would it mean for my life and my future? Telling Mom would make everything too real. Or worse—put her in harm's way. I had to be strong for everyone.

I brushed a stray hair out of my face and headed for my next class. The school day needed to end so I could try my luck with Gwen once more. I hoped I wouldn't get in trouble in the process.

Chapter Fifteen

I knew which way I was headed after the final bell rang. But before that, I intentionally took a long time gathering my things from my locker.

Jane deserved an update even if there was no update at all. Once the hallway cleared and the chatter of students quieted, I walked into the girls' restroom on the first floor. My insides shivered as I laid eyes on Jane, who was waiting for me. She hurried toward me.

"What did Mr. Davis say? Did he say anything about why I was in his chem lab that night?"

Jane spoke so quickly, I had a hard time following.

"He has no idea. Remembers you being a good student. He says he locked his room behind him after school to go make dinner for his mom."

I fidgeted. I had let her down.

"I see," Jane mumbled, looking down to the floor. "Where do we go from here?"

"My mom has done a million investigative reports before. She always pulls the police report. I think I need to get my hands on that. There could be information about possible suspects."

I reached out to comfort her. I stopped myself, unsure of whether touching Jane was even possible.

Would my hand pass through her arm like Casper or something?

I didn't want to weird out either one of us.

Jane giggled when she saw my minor panic. Her gaze met mine once again.

"I know you can do it, Kate," she said. "You're going to find out what happened to me and help make it right."

After we'd said our goodbyes, I booked it toward Main Street, passing the infamous diner and other hot spots. (Note: they weren't hot spots.) I kept up my pace and eventually spotted the KTRD letters.

I had only a few minutes to get my story straight. I planned to go with the same student film club act. I hoped Mom wouldn't catch me showing up again without permission. If she did, I would be toast.

I opened the first set of glass doors and punched the call button as I'd done before.

"Kate? Is that you I see on the security camera?" asked Gwen's nasally voice.

"Sure is, Ms. Gwen. I know I'm not supposed to come down here by myself, but I need to talk to you. May I come in?"

The intercom was silent for a moment. Nervous, I held my breath. Then, the door made a buzzing sound and the lock clicked.

"This had better be good," she cautioned as I entered the lobby. "Don't want to see you wind up grounded." Her eyes narrowed skeptically behind those red-framed glasses, peeking at me over her computer.

"Well, I have kind of a weird request," I began, doing my best to sound confident. "I'm trying to get a film club off the ground at my school."

"Is that so?" Gwen's face softened. "Not too far from TV news, like your mother."

My fingers toyed with my backpack strap. I wanted to smack my own hand away.

"I'm working on a project about safety improvements at Ravendale Middle School since that fire. You know, that one in '95?"

Gwen paused, slowly nodding her head. "Yes, that was awful. I remember how busy this place was that night."

"I can only imagine." I paused, giving Gwen time to process her memories before pressing on. "I was wondering if you have any friends down at City Hall who might be able to pull the original police report."

She stared at me down the barrel of her frames, her eyebrows raised as if she didn't know what to think of the situation. Or of me, a kid, asking her so many nosy questions.

"Maybe," she said. "Why not ask your mom to help? Her name already carries some weight in this town."

"I know. But you can tell how she is. If she knew I was working on this, she'd overstep, and it would become the Maria Silver show." I added a little flourish with my hands to be dramatic. "This is something I want to do on my own."

Gwen shifted in her seat and scooted forward. My last fib seemed to have earned her respect. I realized how ironic that was.

"I'm only agreeing to this because you remind me of someone," she said. "Let me make a few calls. Write your email down for me, and then beat it! Your mom could come through here any minute. I can keep my mouth shut, but I'm not about to tell any lies."

Gwen slid a pad of sticky notes toward me and picked up the receiver of her desk phone. Her long red nails glistened as she dialed a number she clearly had memorized. I jotted down my email address, then mouthed "thank you" before turning and heading back for the front doors.

The info in that police report would point me where to go next. But while I waited, I needed to quiet my growling stomach.

As I strolled down Main Street, I noticed more cars parked along the street than the past few times I'd passed by. It was Friday evening, and apparently, Ravendale residents were out to enjoy it. I decided to stop by the diner to kick off my first weekend in Iowa. I'd avoided getting caught out alone so far that night. Plus, the to-go menu had to have something halfway edible. I didn't know then, but I would need the fuel. My investigation was about to pick up speed. It wasn't going to be a relaxing weekend.

Chapter Sixteen

I rolled over, running my cheek through a pool of my own drool from the night before. I wiped my face with the back of my hand and slapped my cell phone on my nightstand. 8:46 A.M.

It looked like mid-afternoon, judging by the bright sunlight bouncing off my stark white walls. I thought maybe I could talk Mom into picking up some black-out curtains for me that day. Heck, maybe even some paint. It was officially our first weekend in Ravendale. With all that had happened in my first week of school, I was relieved Saturday had arrived—and without a nightmare too.

The trade-off to Mom bringing us to this tiny town was that we would finally have weekends together. I hoped that meant lots of greasy foods, long walks, and scary-movie marathons. I needed a break.

I got out of bed and threw on a pair of wrinkled, black athletic shorts and a gray hoodie. After a quick pit stop in the bathroom to wash my face, brush my teeth, and knot my sleepy frizz into a messy bun on the top of my head, I went into Mom's room. I lifted her heavy white down comforter and crawled in beside her. The movement made Mom stir—or at least start stretching under the blankets.

"Morning already, kiddo?" she grumpily mumbled, massaging her closed eyes with her fists. She reached up overhead and stretched her back, like a baby coming out of its swaddle.

"'Fraid so, Maria," I quipped. "Hey, brunch, then shopping? I need black-out curtains for my white prison cell."

She turned her head toward me and opened her eyes to shoot me an eye roll.

Maybe that's where I learned it.

"At least you said brunch," Mom said. "Give me ten minutes to put myself together." She threw back her blankets and rolled herself out of bed. Her crunchy TV hair always looked hilarious after she'd slept on it. She trudged into her bathroom a few feet away.

I pulled my phone out of my hoodie's front pocket and checked the weather to kill time until Mom was ready. Warm by the afternoon. Sunshine expected. Then, I pulled up my email. What I saw next made my breath catch. I did a double take over my shoulder to make sure Mom wasn't watching.

Sender: Gwen Williams
Subject: Report
Time Sent: Friday, 7:52 P.M.

I clicked.

You're lucky my friend worked late tonight. Scanned and attached. xG

The original 1995 police report from the fire. I couldn't believe it. Gwen's connection had come through much quicker than I'd expected. My finger flew to the attachment, glancing up once more to see the back of Mom's head as she brushed back and forth over her teeth.

Date: October 10, 1995
Time of incident: 5:46 P.M.
Location: Ravendale Middle School, 122 Sherwood Lane

I skimmed over the top section of the report, which contained the nuts and bolts of the incident.

The officer's narrative section had to be where the real meat was. Mom had always said that about police reports anyway. That's where an officer writes, in his or her own words, what happened.

The first few lines described the call that came in from a neighbor across the street who saw smoke coming from the east side of the school. The next bit detailed the emergency response. Ravendale Fire Department, Ravendale Police Department, and Ravendale Ambulance responded, along with some other agencies from surrounding small towns. The fire took hours to extinguish, etc.

My eyes skimmed furiously, looking for the details about Jane.

Suspected human remains.

There it was!
Authorities on the scene found what they believed to be human remains inside the school's destroyed chemistry lab. The writing officer detailed how the medical examiner's office was called to the scene to collect the remains in order to try to identify the victim. He also wrote that the state's fire marshal would arrive the next day to begin the investigation into the cause of the fire.

The officer wrote that around 7 P.M., Mr. and Mrs. Wright arrived at the school, after hearing about the fire on the 6 o'clock news. They reported to officers that Jane hadn't come home that night. She had left a note for them, indicating she planned to visit the diner after school. When dinner time arrived and Jane wasn't home, they called the diner. They were told no one had seen her there. The Wrights didn't have any further details. The officer noted they were tearful and panicked.

There was one final section in the officer's narrative that caught my eye.

> *Officers noticed a child on her bike looking at the burned building around 11:15 P.M. Officers confronted her and learned she was Millie Jefferson, daughter of Scott and Mindy Jefferson.*

I paused to give my brain a beat to catch up.
Jefferson. That name sounded familiar.

I'd heard that name since coming to Ravendale. Maybe I was still half asleep because I couldn't place it. I continued reading the report, hoping it might come to me.

> *Millie was crying. She told a responding officer that she was "really sorry." The officer phoned her parents, who insisted she not speak further. They came to pick her up. They refused detectives' requests to bring her to the station for questioning.*

That was where the report ended. I could've sworn Mom said these kinds of reports usually got filed within a day of something happening.

Why wouldn't Millie's parents cooperate with the police?

I couldn't count on other police documents to explain. The following days, weeks, months, or years of the investigation wouldn't be public record like this because authorities didn't like to share details of ongoing investigations.

The only other public document I figured I could get my hands on would be the state fire marshal's report. I'd seen Mom leave enough of those on our kitchen table over the years to know that much. That report would include a confirmed reason for the fire from the state's top fire investigators. I knew I was pushing my luck, but I hit "reply."

Thank you so much for this, Ms. Gwen. I owe you.
One final favor. In return, I promise to be your summer intern who handles all your busy work.
State fire marshal's report...?

—Kate

I could already picture her face when she opened this email on a Saturday. She would probably curse the day the Sablowsky girls rolled into town. Actually, probably not. It seemed like Gwen was the type to pretend to be inconvenienced but secretly appreciated your persistence. At any rate, I owed it to Jane to try.

The police report had given me a good place to start. Who was Millie? Was she properly investigated? And did she still live in Ravendale?

"Ready, kiddo?" Mom smiled as she pulled a ball of lint from her black leggings. She was out of her bathroom and headed for the hallway.

"Yep," I said, rising from her bed. She didn't have to know *what* I was ready for.

Chapter Seventeen

The clinking of forks against various mismatched plates echoed throughout the diner. Mine stabbed at my scrambled eggs, which I always dipped in ketchup like Mom.

Clearly, *the* diner was *the* place to be on a Saturday morning. People packed into the space like sardines in a can. Warm sunshine poured through the windows. The relatively small restaurant had pale-blue walls and that classic kind of black-and-white checkered floor. You could see back into the packed kitchen, where a group of sweaty guys hurled around order sheets, frying pans, and insults.

A man with a full head of salt-and-pepper hair floated between tables, popping into conversations here and there, calling everyone by name. He looked to be a few years older than Mom and wore a dark-blue bowling shirt with the name "Gil" embroidered over a pocket on his chest. I knew from the name-dropping Mrs. Marsh had done in class that Gil was the owner of the diner.

"Well, if it isn't Maria Silver," he said, stopping to refill Mom's coffee cup. "It's an honor to meet you in person."

Mom was a pro at dealing with weird fan encounters. "That's very kind of you to say," she said, flashing her TV, pearly-white smile. "I've heard about you too. You run a wonderful place here, Gil."

"You flatter me," he said, playfully batting the hand that wasn't holding the coffee pot.

Is he flirting?

I straightened up in my chair to not miss the show.

"And this is my daughter, Kate," Mom said, gesturing to me. "She's in seventh grade."

"Well, Miss Kate, it's not hard to see where your beauty comes from," Gil said, looking back at Mom.

Yep, flirting. Good for him for trying though.

"Happy to have you both here. Can I get you anything else?"

"No, thank you. All set," Mom said.

Mom kept her eyes on Gil as he moved on to the table next to ours. She leaned in and whispered, "Okay, for an Iowa guy, he's kinda cute, right?"

I rolled my eyes. "Mom, don't make me puke. I'm enjoying my breakfast."

That was sort of a lie. The food *was* good, but my fingers were itching to grab for my phone, which I had face-down on the table. I needed to do an internet search for Millie Jefferson, but I had to wait for the right opportunity. Mom had already downed two black coffees and half a glass of water. She was due for a restroom break any second.

"So, kiddo, I know you've met Gwen at work. She's so sweet, and she's been so welcoming. It's hard to believe she can be like that after all she's been through." Mom took a giant bite out of her wheat toast.

I glanced from my phone back to Mom's face. That piqued my interest.

"What she's been through? What do you mean?"

"Oh," Mom gasped, wiping her mouth with the paper napkin from her lap. "Of course, how would you know that? Her son died when he was about your age. Car accident, just awful. Gwen never had any other kids."

My heart sank, enough to put Millie Jefferson on the back burner for a moment. Gwen had mentioned I reminded her of someone when she agreed to help me. She missed her son. I made a mental note that I owed her more than I'd initially thought.

"Yoo-hoo," Mom's voice and waving hand yanked me out of my daydream. "On a happier note, are any of these kids in here from your class?"

I looked around. I spotted Sam sitting with his parents and a teen I assumed was his brother in a corner booth. I didn't want to point Sam out and risk Mom asking if I had a crush on him or something. I did enjoy him as a lab partner but not like *that*.

"Yeah," I said.

"Just yeah? What about that Jane girl you met with for your paper?"

I nearly choked on the piece of turkey bacon I was biting into.

Crap, she remembered.

I had to think fast.

"Yeah, she's in my English class. She's fine. Not someone I see myself being friends with after we leave here." I hoped my response satisfied her. It didn't hurt that it was also entirely accurate. Even so, thinking about Jane for only a second sent that chill up my spine.

"Who says we're leaving here? Remember, I told you Ravendale's going to be different," she said as she took another sip from her coffee cup. She continued as though she hadn't just dropped a bomb at brunch. "I already met our next-door neighbor, by the way. Mrs. Labott. She's old but sweet. She promised to pop over and check on you some evenings for me."

In my disbelief, I skipped past the elderly babysitter bit.

"Mom, you can't be serious. Not leaving Ravendale?! I thought your contract was only three years," I argued, pushing back from the table and reclining in my seat.

"Yeah, but the pay's good. The station seems good. Maybe if we settle down here, you could make some real friends. Who knows, maybe Jane could wind up being the maid of honor in your wedding or something."

Mom wore a teasing smile. She was definitely trying to bug me, and it was working.

"Mom, you have no idea how much I doubt that," I droned.

She must have seen me shoot a longing look at my phone, because she leaned toward me.

"Hey, speaking of weddings, you've been extra married to your phone lately. What gives?"

I avoided eye contact. And I certainly avoided looking at my phone.

"I don't know what you're talking about."

She sat silently for a minute.

"Okay." She paused. "Honesty is our thing though."

"Oh my gosh, Mom! I *know!*" I slapped my hand to my forehead.

Mom smiled, satisfied with herself, and scooted her chair back. She pointed at the bathroom and said she would be right back. No sooner had she left the table than I whipped out my phone. I punched Millie's name into a search browser, along with Ravendale.

Reverie Day Spa, Ravendale, Iowa.

"Hey, tell your Mom no charge this time. Think of it as a welcome-to-Ravendale present." I jumped and flipped my phone upside down on the table again. The voice was Gil's. He was back at our table with a big grin plastered on his face.

"Um, thanks. That's really nice of you," I said. Then I got an idea. "Actually, uh, Gil?"

"Yeah?"

"What do you know about the Jeffersons?"

"The Jeffersons?" he responded. "Well, I'll put it this way. About two-thirds of the people in this town work for them at Jefferson Foods, the canning facility. The other third grows the food for the canning. Yeah, Scott and Mindy are a powerhouse in these parts."

"What about their daughter, Millie?" I asked.

"Nice enough gal. Didn't want to take up the family business with her brothers but owns a pretty ritzy spa not too far from here. Might make for a fun girls' day!"

Gil piled Mom's and my plates on his arms, nodded, and headed back for the kitchen.

I sat staring at the tablecloth, lost in my thoughts. Millie's family practically ran this town. If their daughter had something to do with Jane's murder, they probably had the power to make any evidence or investigation disappear. I had to find a way to convince Mom to go to Millie's spa and fast. I needed to meet her and ask her some questions.

A few minutes later, Mom returned to the table, wiping her wet hands on her leggings. She started digging in her purse.

"It's okay, Mom," I said. "Gil said there's no bill today. A welcome-to-Ravendale or something. I don't know."

Her cheeks blushed. She looked back to where Gil hovered at the counter and waved.

"Well, that's extremely kind of him, isn't it? Are you ready to roll?"

I stood, sliding my phone back into my pocket.

There was a home-goods shop a few blocks down the road from the diner, so we decided to head that way on foot. As we walked, Mom told me about her co-anchor and some of the funny things they say to each other during commercial breaks. Her stories made it obvious she was happy here. I didn't let that bother me too much, since I had to stay focused on what I'd set out to do.

The whole stop at the store took five minutes, tops. The shop's bell jingled as we walked back out onto the sidewalk, my black-out curtains in a bag in my hand.

"Hey, Mom, do we have any other plans for today?" I asked.

"Nope." Mom paused, then smiled. "Well, I guess it's Shabbat, so that means we ought to focus on taking it easy."

She gave my arm a little love punch.

"Funny you should say that," I began, keeping my eyes pointed at the ground. "What do you think about getting facials?"

My suggestion literally stopped her in her tracks. I turned around to look at her.

"But you hate that stuff," Mom said, looking confused. "You think it's too girly."

"Maybe I changed my mind," I said, shifting my weight nervously from one foot to the other. "You know how middle school is. Kids with bad skin get teased and stuff."

"Hang on a sec." Mom's tone changed. "Is somebody picking on you?"

She raised her voice and put her hand on my shoulder. "Look at me, Kate. *Is someone being mean to you?*"

"Of course not, Mom. Jeez. Take a breath." I rolled my eyes and raised my voice too.

Why does she have to make this so hard?

"I just want to take care of my skin, okay? I actually have a place in mind."

Mom narrowed her eyes. She wasn't completely buying into

my act, but she decided to at least run with it. I knew that because she started walking again.

"Fine. But so we're clear, you know if any kid says even one mean thing to you, you have to tell me, right? Because I'd take them down."

I grabbed her hand. "Seriously, somebody ought to study you."

I pulled out my phone to pretend I was looking up the spa's address. In reality, I had it memorized. I had no idea what I was about to experience there. It was possible I was mere minutes away from coming face-to-face with Jane's murderer.

Chapter Eighteen

S ome kind of flowery smell punched me in the face as I walked into Reverie Day Spa. The walls were stark white and seemed to flow right into the gray-white flooring. It was the modern kind, made to look like wood but wasn't wood at all. There was also some kind of strange wind-chime music softly playing from a speaker. If the tones were meant to be calming, they weren't working.

"Welcome, ladies," sang a high school-aged girl softly. She had bronzed, spray-tanned skin and a ponytail that was as straight as an arrow. She wore a black fitted top with a white name tag that said "Kelly." I could almost see my reflection in her clear lip gloss. "What brings you in today?"

"Facials, I guess," my mom said in a dry tone. She shot me a suspicious look.

"Wonderful." Kelly smiled, still in her hushed spa voice. She typed something into the keyboard in front of her with pink manicured nails.

"Ah, looks like we only have one of our girls performing that service today. We can get you both in but only one at a time. Who would like to go first?" She looked up to await our response.

"Go ahead, Mom," I said, nudging her toward the door behind the desk, where I imagined the spa rooms were. "I don't mind waiting."

The lights would be dim back there, and Mom would be snoring before the poor aesthetician ever got started. I didn't want to wait another hour for answers for Jane.

"You sure, kiddo?" Mom asked as she adjusted her purse strap. She was used to me being snarky and was probably waiting on some kind of rude joke. Not this time.

"Yeah, go for it," I said. "Shoo!"

"Aww, that's sweet," said Kelly, bringing her hand to her heart in an insincere way. She made eye contact with Mom, then pointed toward the door behind her. "Just head back through that door, and the women's locker room is on the left. You'll find your spa robe and sandals there."

"Alrighty," Mom said to us both. She walked past the desk, glancing over her shoulder with concern one final time. When she opened the back door, the wind-chime music played even louder.

I couldn't waste any time. Once the door closed behind Mom, I made my move.

"Umm, excuse me? I'm wondering if the owner is around today," I said to Kelly, whose attention had already returned to the spa computer.

"Yes, she is," Kelly responded with a polite smile, though she immediately returned to scrolling.

"Uh, okay, great." I paused, hoping she would catch my obvious hint. "Would you mind getting her for me?"

That got her attention.

"Sure, wait here," she said with a hint of irritation. She

clicked the computer mouse once more then disappeared through a door on the far right side of the spa lobby. There wasn't wind chime music that time. I figured that had to be the business office.

After about thirty seconds, the door opened. Kelly walked out first, followed by a curvy woman also dressed in black. She had the same shade of spray-tanned skin with short, heavily high-lighted hair styled into relaxed beach waves. It had to be her.

"Hi, there," she said. Her voice was a bit huskier than I had anticipated. "I'm Millie. What can I do for you?" She meandered behind the desk until she stood directly in front of me. If she really was Jane's killer, it seemed cruel that she passed each day in a place dedicated to peace and relaxation. My fists tightened.

"Uhh, I'm Kate Sablowsky. I'm trying to start a student film club at Ravendale Middle School, and I was hoping you could help me with something." I tried to keep my voice as calm as I could. I didn't have my backpack on me, so I couldn't properly sell the film-kid bit with my GoPro. I was winging it.

"I'm not that big on on-camera stuff." Millie chuckled, as though trying to let me down as politely as possible.

"Well, you wouldn't have to be on-camera," I said. "I'm looking for some information to get me started. I'm working on a project about safety improvements at the school since the fire in 1995. Mrs. Nettles shared a few names with me of students she remembered from that time. You were one of them."

I could feel my cheeks flush slightly with my blatant lie.

"She did?" Millie asked, shooting a quick look at me, then at the front-desk girl. Her expression appeared more concerned than curious.

"Kelly, why don't you go grab lunch a little early today?" she suggested. It was a nice offer, but her tone was firm.

"Okay," Kelly said as she grabbed her wallet from the desk's top drawer and headed for the front door. She didn't seem like she needed to be told twice to take a break. Millie waited until the door clicked closed.

"What exactly did Mrs. Nettles tell you?" Millie didn't sound angry, but she didn't exactly sound friendly either.

I started to fidget with the seams of my shorts below the counter's view.

"Nothing really," I said, a bit defensive. "She just named ten or so people who came to mind as being students at the time."

"Well, that was a long time ago," Millie said. She didn't continue, probably hoping I'd pick up on her disinterest. I knew I'd have to work for the information she gave me. What I said next was going to get under her skin.

"Mrs. Nettles said she'd heard you came by the school late the night of the fire. May I ask why?"

Millie didn't say anything for a moment. Her dark brown eyes stared into mine. She was visibly uncomfortable. I worried I might've gone a step too far.

"I don't know what that has to do with safety improvements at the school," she said in a hushed and irritated tone. "I'm sure she told you I didn't cooperate with the police, but that isn't true. I had nothing to tell them. I was at my tennis lesson when the fire started, close to six that night. And a lot of people saw me there."

Millie sounded guilty, like she was trying to throw me off. I'd never asked her for an alibi.

"If that's true, why did you tell an officer at the scene that you were sorry?"

Oh no.

My own words nearly made me gasp out loud. The accusation had slipped out before I could stop myself. If I'd thought I'd overstepped before, I had truly ruined everything. All the blood rushed from my face.

A few seconds passed as Millie seemed to choose her next

words carefully. When she finally spoke, she almost hissed. A whisper packed with venom.

"Ms. Sablowsky, I don't have anything else to say to you. I ask you to kindly have a seat, wait for your mom to finish her service, then go. Have a nice day."

With that, she turned and strode quickly out of the front lobby and back through the door to the business office. It shut behind her with a bang.

My jaw was still hanging open. I couldn't believe what had just happened. Millie had a secret, and I'd called her out.

I blew it.

That was *not* how Mom spoke with her story sources, even when she knew they were holding something back.

At that moment, I felt Jane next to me. She wasn't *really* there, but that familiar chill washed over me. I'd let her down and she might never be free of our school. My stomach twisted.

At this point, what more do I have to lose?

I ran behind the spa's desk and grasped a pen and piece of paper. I scribbled a message as quickly as I could before Millie might return.

If you change your mind.
309-555-7845.
—Kate Sablowsky

REVERIE
DAY SPA

I set down the pen, then raced to the front door before I could do any more damage. On the way, I sent a quick text to Mom, telling her I felt a little sick from my breakfast and would be waiting for her in the car.

I knew then Millie Jefferson was my prime suspect. My chest tightened as I came to the terrifying conclusion: The last person to wind up on her list could've been Jane. Was I on Millie's list now too?

Chapter Nineteen

I woke up long before my alarm went off Monday morning. I hadn't slept much. The rest of the weekend had been a blur. I stared up at my ceiling, playing back the moments I could remember as I waited for 6:45 A.M.

Mom had returned to the car after her facial with glowing, clear skin. Her cheeks were a bit red from all the products and the wiping that went into that service. At least that's what she'd said. She didn't appear to believe me that I wasn't feeling well, but she didn't push the issue. She kept sneaking peeks at me out of the corner of her eyes on the way home. We'd camped out on the couch pretty much the rest of the day watching movies, only taking a break to hang my new black-out curtains.

Sunday was more of the same. More scary movies, more pizza, more sweats, and no showers. With the exception of a quick hour dedicated to homework, it would've been a perfect first Mom/Kate weekend. That, and if I hadn't been holding so much back from her.

"You sure you're okay, kiddo?" Mom had asked me a few times. Each time, I nodded or told her to stop being a worrywart.

The truth was, not telling her about Jane, Millie, or the fire was eating me up inside, but I couldn't risk it. I still wasn't ready to deal with whatever having Bubbe's gift meant. And I didn't want Mom to stop me from doing what I had to do to help Jane.

If only Bubbe was here to help me figure things out.

It seemed like the least she could do, after sticking me with her gift that wasn't a gift.

I wound up turning off my alarm at 6:40. There was no use in waiting. I tried to breathe deeply in the shower and let the steam calm my nerves. I had a lot of explaining to do when I got to school. Jane would be waiting for me, and I had only disappointing news. She had trusted me to help her find peace, and I was clearly not capable of measuring up.

I threw on a pair of jeans and a T-shirt, breathing out a "good enough" kind of sigh as I caught a glimpse of my reflection in the mirror. I let my hair air dry as I ate my Pop-Tarts and chugged a glass of orange juice. By the time I'd eaten, packed a lunch, and stuffed my backpack, my blond frizz was dry enough to pull into a ponytail.

I needed an umbrella for my walk to school with the gray sky shaking loose a light rainfall. The absence of the sun, coupled with the rain, made it almost chilly. The few moments I wasn't thinking of my upcoming conversation with Jane, I regretted choosing jeans that were now damp at the heels.

The rain made my morning text to Mom easy:

Washed away by the floodwaters. Bye.

As usual, her response was equally horrible:

You'll wind up in the ocean at some point. Text me when, and I'll plan a beach trip.

Ha ha, very funny, Mom.

The chill hit me like a freight train when I opened the school doors. I didn't have the chance to react with the students and teachers rushing by me, chatting and walking. But by the time I reached the seventh-grade hallway, there she was.

Jane looked perfectly put-together, as always, standing in front of the big window at the end of the hall. There wasn't a wrinkle in her gray sweater. Her arms were wrapped around her chemistry book, clutching it to her chest. She offered a tiny smile as a greeting. Some would find the whole image eerie, if they could see her. But on this day, I just found it sad. I didn't have the news that she so desperately waited for. I smiled back and glanced at the clock hanging above a section of lockers. She seemed to understand that I would meet her at a better time when others weren't around.

I made my way to my locker, entered my combination into the lock, and clicked the door open. A white note card at the base of my locker stared back at me. I didn't own any note cards. My heart beat faster. There was writing on it.

I bent down and scooped up the note, looking around to be sure no one was watching. I was sure I looked as pale as Jane. The writing was messy and rushed.

STOP ASKING QUESTIONS.
YOU DON'T KNOW WHAT YOU'RE
DOING.

My breathing stopped. The hallway spun. I sank down onto my bottom at the base of my locker and read the note several more times. It was a threat. A threat to stop asking questions about the fire.

"Kate, you okay?" Sam walked up beside me, his blue backpack slung over his shoulder. He looked worried. I wondered how much attention I'd drawn to myself.

"Yeah, fine. I'm totally fine," I said, attempting to shake off the bomb I'd just discovered and get out of the way. I grabbed the open locker door and used it to pull myself up, even though it swung this way and that.

"You sure you don't need anything?" he asked, looking around, as more students started to notice my little episode.

"I'm sure. I'll see you in chem." It was a polite, Midwestern way of saying *beat it*, and he got the hint.

Millie. It had to be Millie. Who else would want me to shut up enough to leave a threatening note?

I wondered how she'd even gotten access to the school over the weekend. It paid to live in a small town—especially with a well-known last name.

I slammed my locker door shut and stifled a scream. Jane's face was right behind the door.

"I know you can't look at me or answer out loud, but nod or shake your head," she said. "Are you okay?"

I nodded and shot her a quick look that tried to say I'd tell her what had happened soon. The bottom line was, I had to be getting closer to an answer for Jane. Somebody, probably Millie, was scared. What I was digging up was dangerous information, and I wondered if the risks were worth it. I folded the note card in half and stuffed it in my pocket.

RINGGGG.

Mrs. Marsh wore a large gold shawl wrapped around her body and tossed over her right shoulder. Some of her curls were caught inside it. She looked like she was channeling the drama teacher in the original *High School Musical*, another one of Mom's random favorite movies.

"Good morning, Oliver. That must be a new Vikings shirt! We match in our team colors today," Mrs. Marsh sang, clasping her hands with glee. "And, sweet Kate, how are you on this rainy day?"

"Umm, good," I managed, again caught off-guard by Mrs. Marsh's vivacious attitude day in, day out. Then, an idea hit me. I stopped walking toward my desk and turned to her.

"Actually, I'm not great. Bad breakfast burrito this morning."

"You poor dear!" Mrs. Marsh brought both of her hands to my cheeks, like I was her baby. "Would you like me to call for the nurse?"

"No, no, I'm okay," I said, as I tried to shake my head, but it was lodged in place by her palms. "Just a trip to the bathroom, if that's alright with you."

"Of course, dear." She released her hands and offered me another genuine smile before turning to greet the other students.

That was easier than I'd thought.

The hallways were empty as students settled into their first classes of the day. It was only the chill that accompanied me to the girls' restroom.

Jane greeted me as soon as the heavy wooden door swung closed behind me.

"Hi, Kate. What happened out there?" The fluorescent light reflected off Jane's pale skin. Her smile was warm, even though the air surrounding us felt so cold. She fidgeted with the corner of her chemistry book that was wearing out.

"This." I handed her the note card.

Jane's expression hardened as she read the message.

"I think it's from Millie," I added.

Jane's jaw dropped and her eyes widened.

"Millie? Millie Jefferson from school? What are you talking about?"

"I promise, I'm digging like crazy to find you answers. And it seems like this weekend, my digging struck a nerve."

Jane sat down on the hard bathroom floor and folded her legs like an eager kindergartener.

"Catch me up."

I got down on the ground and joined her, hoping no one would walk in. I recounted the roundabout way I'd been able to get a copy of the original police report and how Millie had been at the school late the night of the fire. How she didn't answer the police officers' questions.

"She what?" Jane exclaimed, her voice echoing off the stalls.

"So, you remember her, then?" I asked, clinging to a sudden shred of hope.

"Millie and I weren't really friends. I remember we sometimes felt a little competitive with each other. But I would never have thought she would take it this far."

"You think it's possible that Millie started the fire—or that she locked you inside the chem lab?" I asked.

Obviously, Millie was the primary suspect in my mind, but hearing Jane mention their competitive relationship strengthened my hunch.

Jane's expression was serious. She nodded her head, making her brown bob dance.

"How old would she be now?" Jane asked. Like me, math didn't seem to be her strong suit.

"At least 37," I said. "She owns a spa in town. Practically ran me out of it when I started asking questions."

"How do we force her to tell the truth?" Jane asked as she brought her hand to her temple.

BAM.

The bathroom door swung open. A girl with dark hair rushed

in, stopping when she saw me on the floor. She must have been an eighth grader since I didn't recognize her from any of my classes.

"Are you okay?" she asked.

"Yeah, just lightheaded. Had to sit for a minute," I spat out. It was starting to scare me how good I'd become at lying for Jane's sake.

I glanced back to where Jane had been sitting, but she was gone. She had vanished, taking the chilly air with her.

"Want me to get the nurse?" the girl asked.

"No, I'm good," I said as I pushed myself up and onto my knees. "I think I'll head back to class."

As I stood, my phone buzzed in my back pocket. A text from a number I didn't recognize with a Ravendale area code.

> Leslie Park. 9 p.m. — MJ

I gasped when I saw Millie Jefferson's initials. The texter had to be her.

The eighth grader stared at me, obviously bewildered by the weirdo in the bathroom.

I read the message three more times to be certain I wasn't imagining it. Millie wanted to meet, despite our confrontation over the weekend.

Is she ready to come clean? Is she going to confess to murder? Or is she planning something to stop me from asking any more questions?

I shuddered because there wasn't really a choice. I had to be smart, but I also had to be at that park. With a deep breath, I typed my reply.

> I'll be there.

I looked up and realized the eighth grader had never gone into a bathroom stall. She lingered there, a concerned look on her face. My mind raced, spinning with thoughts of what I was up against that night.

"Bad breakfast burrito," I managed, immediately wanting to disappear from embarrassment.

Smooth.

I beelined for the door and didn't look back to see her reaction. I had far bigger fish to fry.

A possible murder suspect wanted to meet with me alone and after dark. I had so much to do to get ready.

Chapter Twenty

I thought about that scene in *Home Alone* where the main character, Kevin, ate his dinner, waiting for the burglars to arrive. Like him, I sat at our small, circular table at the nook in our kitchen. There was a cheese and turkey sandwich on a plate in front of me, but I couldn't bring myself to eat more than a bite. My stomach was in knots thinking of what was to come.

The letter I'd written Mom sat next to my plate. It was part of my plan to protect myself, and it was simple. My letter began with an apology for breaking her rule not to venture out on my own. I explained I was going to meet Millie Jefferson at Leslie Park at 9 P.M. I detailed how she was a suspect in the death of Jane Wright in 1995. Of course, I didn't mention a ghost was the one who sent me on this mission in the first place. If I didn't make it back by the time Mom got home from the station, the letter would be there and she would know to call for help. If I was safe, I'd destroy the letter before she saw it.

I'd made sure my GoPro was fully charged. I planned to wear my baggy black sweatshirt and hide it in the front pocket. The sound would be muffled, but if she was to confess, I might be able to capture it and turn it over to the police. Plus, using the camera would keep my cell phone free if I needed to call for help.

I tapped my phone's screen for what was probably the hundredth time.

8:27.

I needed to leave in about eight minutes to make it to Leslie Park on foot by 9 o'clock. I'd mapped it out and memorized the route after school. I ripped off a piece of turkey hanging from the side of my sandwich and lifted it to my mouth. I chewed but couldn't concentrate on the taste.

Am I about to get hurt? Will I ever see my mom again?

There was no use trying to pass the time. I needed to leave right then. The waiting was torture.

As I scooted my chair back, I heard a firm knock at the front door.

I jumped with such force that I knocked my plate and the partially eaten sandwich onto the floor. A knock may have seemed harmless if I wasn't preparing to meet a murder suspect after dark.

Terrified, I dove under the table. I took a shaky breath as wild thoughts ran a marathon in my head.

Is it Millie? Is the park too public? Did she come to finish me off here with no witnesses?

KNOCK, KNOCK, KNOCK.

I leaned out from under the table until I had a line of sight to the front door. A shadowy figure was bent over, trying to peek through the narrow window next to the door. My heart pounded faster as I tried to make myself smaller. I couldn't make out much as the window was covered by a thin curtain for privacy. Thank goodness it was, so the shadow couldn't spot me.

"KATE?" a female voice called out.

I jumped again. Hiding wouldn't get me very far. I took off like a determined toddler on my hands and knees, crawling to the window on the other side of the table. It had a view of the front of the house.

I pushed myself up into a crouching position, peeking my eyes up to the window.

It wasn't Millie.

Chapter Twenty One

I knew the investigation into Jane's death was getting to me, but my reaction to the knocking at the door was proof I'd been pushed to my limit.

An elderly woman with tight white curls and a red sweater clutched a plate of cookies and tried to peek in the window by the door.

Mrs. Labott from next door.

I took a massive deep breath and allowed my shoulders to unclench. I scurried to the front door and turned the knob to open it.

"Hi! I'm sorry to keep you waiting, Mrs. Labott," I said, forcing a giant smile on my face. The quicker we chatted, the quicker she would leave and let me get on my way to meet Millie.

"It's okay, dear," she crooned. "I was worried I was going to have to call your mother if you didn't answer. She asked me to pop over from time to time to check on you. No offense to you young people, but you can never be sure if you are where you say you'll be. Just looking at you, though, I can tell you're a good girl."

I felt a wave of guilt wash over me.

If only she knew where I'm headed.

"Yep, just a quiet night in!" My fake smile weakened. In my head, my Pinocchio nose grew a foot.

"Anyway, I made these for you girls," Mrs. Labott said with a smile, handing over the plate. "If there's anything you need, I'm just next door. Goodnight, sweetheart."

She turned and began her walk back home, which was really more of a shuffle in tan loafers.

Close one.

I checked the time again. 8:32.

I decided to sit tight a minute—long enough for Mrs. Labott to get home. I patted my pockets, double checking that I'd remembered my phone and camera. Then, I stepped out into the darkness.

With each step, I wished Jane could come with me. She made me feel stronger, more confident. She believed in me. I wished I could believe in myself that same way.

As I crossed onto a neighborhood street, a passing car made me jump. There were streetlights scattered around the block, but the dark sky made it hard to see my surroundings. I needed to get a hold of myself. I decided to focus on my breathing. In and out. In and out. That only lasted about half a block.

THUMP, THUMP, THUMP.

My heart slammed in my chest as I heard footsteps behind me, pounding against the sidewalk. I grasped my phone tighter and tried to subtly glance over my shoulder.

Is Millie following me? Is this a trap?

Out of the corner of my eye, I saw the thumps were coming from a pair of well-loved Nike tennis shoes. They belonged to a young boy in jeans and a Minnesota Vikings hoodie. His textured hair was short with a fade on the sides, and he seemed about my age. With a sigh of relief, I offered a polite wave so I wouldn't seem awkward.

My wave stopped him in his tracks. He didn't return it. He stood still as a look of fear crossed his face.

I turned back around and continued walking in the direction of the park, so I wouldn't make the situation worse.

Great work, Kate. You were scared thirty seconds ago and now you're scaring another innocent kid.

Suddenly, a chill coursed through me. My shoulders quivered. I looked up at a branch, hanging over the sidewalk, but it wasn't moving. There was no wind at all.

It can't be.

I spun around to look at the boy once more, but he was gone. My breathing quickened again. I hadn't heard him run away.

Is he like Jane? Is that why he freaked out when I waved?

With a shallow breath, I answered my own question.

He assumed I couldn't see him.

I looked both ways to be sure I hadn't missed something. That was just what I needed heading into a meeting with a murder suspect.

How many people do I come across on any given day that aren't "here?" How do I tell the difference?

I couldn't get bogged down by these thoughts. Not at that moment. I had somewhere to be.

When I arrived at Leslie Park, my eyes frantically searched for Millie between forced deep and even breaths. I'd already experienced several scares and our meeting hadn't even happened yet. It seemed I was the first to arrive. I scanned the area for a possible escape if I needed one.

I stood next to the park's sign, illuminated by a streetlight. From there, the ground slanted downward, then upward again toward the playground. It looked almost like a small valley. I'd watched enough scary movies to know you didn't want to be climbing uphill while being chased. Too easy to fall. Plus, the grass was probably still slick from the morning rain.

Across from the playground was a basketball court, probably about as far away as I could throw a ball. Weeds poked through cracks in the court's surface, and another streetlight shone behind the far hoop. Within the light's beam sat a park bench.

Bingo.

Again, my scary-movie knowledge reminded me to stay in a well-lit area, if possible.

I timed out deep inhales and exhales in the rhythm of my steps as I walked toward the park bench. I continued to scan the area and glanced back over both shoulders. When I reached the bench, I pulled out my cell phone to check the time.

8:55.

How had only twenty minutes passed since I had been sitting at home? Time seemed to move in slow motion. I wondered if that was how Jane felt all of the time.

My timed breaths came to an abrupt halt when I saw a small black Mercedes turn onto the street next to the park. I followed its bright beams with my eyes as it pulled close to the curb on the far side of the street. The car was only twenty or thirty steps away from the park bench. If Millie planned to make a quick getaway, she'd chosen her parking spot well. My body tensed. I reached into my front pocket and punched the record button on my GoPro. My other hand grasped my phone firmly.

The car's bright beams clicked off, and the driver's side door swung open. Millie stepped out in blue jeans and a faded gray sweatshirt. Her perfectly styled beach waves had gone completely flat. As she approached, I noticed she didn't have any makeup on her face. As a spa person, I imagined that was rare for her.

She didn't offer a smile. In fact, it was the opposite. She had tear streaks running down her face. Her skin was tinged red as though she had been crying for a while. My hand, tightly clasped around my phone, loosened.

Chapter Twenty Two

Millie sat next to me on the bench. Her fist squeezed a wet tissue. She was shaking. She sniffed loudly, the way somebody does after a good cry.

Millie hadn't greeted me. She hadn't said one word. The white tips of her French manicure glimmered under the street-light. Her breaths wheezed in and out of her runny nose. The lingering silence made me want to cringe, but I wasn't going to be the one to break it. I shifted in my seat as my imagination ran wild, picturing Millie at the scene of the crime.

Mom always said one of the worst mistakes journalists could make in interviews was to fill the silence. Most people naturally wanted to do that to avoid any awkwardness.

"That's when your subject is most likely to share something important," she'd said. "You just have to wait."

And so I did. I picked at a loose string on the sleeve of my sweatshirt. Fireflies twirled above the grass across the basketball court. Millie watched them, interrupting their dance every few seconds with a sniffle.

At least half a minute had passed. As the seconds ticked by, I became less and less afraid. Millie didn't seem like an angry villain. She seemed broken. But she definitely had a secret.

At last, she drew a deep breath. I straightened up, my back pressed firmly against the bench. I moved my right hand to rest on the front of my sweatshirt pocket, then subtly patted my camera to make sure it was doing its job.

"I do have something to say about the day Jane Wright died," Millie finally whispered to the air, avoiding my face. I got the impression she was going to confess something to the world. I just happened to be there to hear it.

"What is it, Millie?" I asked as softly as I could, hoping to offer encouragement.

"Jane and I were competitive back then." Millie's eyes glazed over as the memories seemed to return to her. "We were the top scorers in our class. We were the only Alto IIs in the school choir. It wasn't crazy that we wanted to outshine one another."

I wanted to come right out and shout, SO YOU KILLED HER?! And then threatened another twelve-year-old decades later?!

But I heard Mom's voice again in my brain. *Don't fill the silence. She's about to say something important.* I chose to nod instead.

"We were chem partners in Mr. Davis's class. Science was one area where Jane couldn't touch me. She needed tutoring. I didn't. I just understood it better." Millie paused. "Then, that day in October came."

I was glued to her words. I leaned closer.

"What happened?" I asked.

"We got our chem tests back. I don't remember what the test was on. I don't remember much at all, really. I've tried to block so much of it out. I do remember Jane got a ninety-eight. Mr. Davis smiled when he set her paper in front of her. He congratulated her. He said all her hard work had paid off."

Millie looked at me.

"I don't know how much you know about Mr. Davis. I know he's still there."

Well, Jane is too. Go on.

"He knew I was the best student in his class. He knew my reputation was everything to me." A fresh tear rolled down Millie's cheek. I knew her sadness wasn't about any stupid score on any stupid test. It was probably about whatever came after.

"He set my exam down on my desk and had the gall to say out loud, 'C-minus. Disappointing, Ms. Jefferson.' And everyone heard. My cheeks turned beet red. It was *humiliating*." There was a hint of a snarl in Millie's last word.

I didn't have to wait for a silent pause this time. Her pace quickened.

"When class ended that day, I didn't say a word to anyone. I wanted to get even with him. I fished out my pair of scissors from my pencil bag. When I walked past Mr. Davis's desk to head for the hallway, I snipped the phone line on his desk phone. The cord always hung over the front of his desk and plugged into the wall. Kids tripped on it all the time."

Millie took a breath and looked down at her hands.

"No one saw me do it. I just wanted to ruin his day the way he'd ruined mine. He'd go to pick up his phone to call the front office for something dumb, and he wouldn't be able to. He'd be angry."

Then it hit me like a semitruck. I drew a breath in but no air came.

The phone line was cut in his classroom. Jane couldn't call for help when the fire broke out.

Millie must've recognized the realization on my face. She collapsed forward, her elbows came to her knees, and she sobbed into her open hands. Her shoulders heaved with grief.

I lifted my hand from where it rested near my camera and

brought it to Millie's back. I gently rubbed in slow circles the way Mom did to me when I was upset.

I wasn't sitting next to a murderer. I wasn't in any danger. Millie meant to upset Mr. Davis. She didn't mean to cut off Jane from outside help. Rivalry or not, she wasn't capable of that.

"I didn't mean for it to happen," Millie moaned between uncontrollable sobs. "I was a stupid kid. Never in a million years would I have cut that phone line if I'd known..."

She couldn't complete her sentence. I finished it for her silently in my mind.

That Jane would've needed to call for help.

"I know. It's okay," I whispered. I didn't want to rub salt in her lingering wound, but I needed more answers. I decided to push a tiny bit further.

"Why didn't you agree to police questioning?" I asked.

She looked up at me and wiped her eyes again with her tissue. I brought my hand back to my lap but kept my eyes locked on her.

"I wanted to tell them the truth. I really did." Millie sounded like she was pleading. "I felt so guilty for what I'd done. But by now, you know who my parents are and what a big deal they are in town. I told them what had happened, and they called their lawyers right away. The lawyers instructed me not to say anything. I guess over the following weeks, the police never dug up any evidence on me, and that was the end of that."

Millie paused.

"It doesn't change how I feel now, though, even after all these years." She hung her head.

"Millie, you can't blame yourself for what happened," I assured her. "You didn't start that fire. You didn't know Jane was going to be in trouble."

"Then, why do I feel like I can still see her face everywhere?" she asked before, unexpectedly, letting out a deep chuckle. "I'm sorry. You're just a kid. This is really heavy. I don't know why I'm dumping all this on you."

As she laughed at herself, Millie wiped the tears from underneath her eyes, shaking off the sadness from her unwelcome trip down memory lane.

"Actually, I get it more than you know," I said, staring blankly off into space.

At least about seeing Jane's face everywhere.

Later when I walked home, another chill pulsed down my spine. It wasn't triggered by Jane's presence at school or any unexpected guests on my route.

If Millie didn't leave me that note in my locker... who did?

Chapter Twenty Three

T hick, black smoke covered the chem lab, making it impossible to breathe. I tried to inhale quicker, sharper, hoping to catch whatever air in the room was left before it was gone. A shelf collapsed as the orange flames climbed rows of books. The sound made me jump, as though my life wasn't already at risk. The lab tables and stools burned as glass shattered.

I ran to the wooden door.

I used what oxygen I had to shout, "PLEASE HELP ME. HELLO? PLEASE HELP ME!" I stopped when coughs consumed my lungs. The fit threw me to my knees before the door. I raised my fists and pounded against it with everything I had. No answer.

Was there another way out? I had never looked before, but I knew I had to try. There were two windows, one against the far left wall, behind the lab desks, and one straight ahead, next to Mr. Davis's desk. I stumbled there, coughs erupting from my chest. My body coursed with adrenaline. I picked up Mr. Davis's rolling desk chair and hurled it at the window. The metal legs clattered against the double-plated glass and smashed to the floor. It was no use.

I grabbed his desk phone and picked up the receiver. No dial tone. Dead. The cord was cut, just like Millie had said.

"Kate, you can't give up!"

I spun around. Was someone there? Between my coughs, I heard a voice shouting to me from the hallway. Fighting the urge to faint, I ran clumsily for the locked door, bumping into debris as I went.

"PLEASE! PLEASE! I'M–" I couldn't finish my thought. The coughing ate my words. I hurled my body into the door and brought my face to the pane of glass to get a glimpse of my savior. I wiped it free of soot.

It was Millie in the hallway. She looked like she did the day I met her at the spa, dressed in all black. Her highlighted beach waves shone beneath the hallway lights.

"Millie! Let me out!" I screamed.

Suddenly, everything around me froze. The crackling of the fire and the explosions of chem supplies ceased. Everything was silent. There was just her and me, separated by the door.

"I can't do that, Kate," Millie said softly, a single tear rolling down her cheek. "I wasn't there that night. You know that now. Only Jane remembers. You have to help Jane remember."

Then like a roar, the flames sprang back to life around me. Another glass beaker shattered in the chaos. I collapsed.

* * *

I FLOPPED ONTO MY SIDE VIOLENTLY, AND THE IMPACT jolted me awake. My sweat-logged hair slapped my face as I looked in every direction to be sure the flames were gone. I sat up and took a few slow, steadying breaths. They didn't do much to slow my heart rate. I blinked my tired eyes.

Was it true, what Millie had said in my dream?

It was just that: a dream. Millie hadn't actually told me in person that it was my responsibility to help Jane remember what happened. The assumption she and I already had all the information we needed to piece the mystery together was impossible.

I wound up shuffling down the hall to Mom's room and snuggling under her big down comforter. My mind continued to race. I tossed and turned, equal parts nervous, excited, and heartbroken to update Jane on what I'd learned.

The fact I had an update at all was positive news. I hadn't been able to offer Jane that in what felt like forever. Millie's story cleared her as a suspect of the fire, but her actions may have contributed to Jane not being able to get help that October night. I wouldn't know Jane's reaction until I delivered the update in person.

Chapter Twenty-Four

The seventh-grade hallway wasn't busy, but it wasn't empty either. Some students were digging in their lockers, others sat on the floor finishing last night's homework.

I was still so out of sorts from my talk with Millie and the awful nightmare that followed, my morning text to Mom was only a thumbs-up emoji. I didn't have it in me to be clever.

I arrived about twenty minutes earlier than usual. I wanted to talk to Jane before first period. My brain was mush, and my breaths were sharp and shallow. I needed to offload what I'd learned.

The library seemed like the best spot. I couldn't picture the flannel-and-crop-top types logging study time there outside school hours. Hopefully, it would be empty, like when we worked on our English paper.

While I didn't see Jane, I felt her chill as I approached the thick wooden doors to the library. With each step, the temperature dropped a few degrees. I trusted she was close by.

With a thud, the wooden doors swung closed behind me. Direct morning sunlight illuminated the stained glass, and the bright colors bounced off the rows of dark books before me.

"Anything I can help you with, miss?"

I must have jumped about a foot into the air. I turned to my left, where the library's check-out desk sat. Behind it was an elderly man with gray, neatly combed hair, thick clear-framed glasses, and a navy bowtie. A lint-free navy sweater with big buttons wrapped around his white-collared shirt. The man was straight out of the movie *Up* but slimmer, fitter. More energetic. He had a kind smile, though I couldn't tell if his teeth were real or dentures.

"Umm, no thanks," I said, slowing my walk toward the rows of books while I tried to drum up an excuse for what I was up to.

"Don't usually get too many visitors before school hours," the man said through his smile. His voice was kind of creaky and crackly, like some old people's were. But it was also high-pitched and chipper. "I'm Edgar Everett, school librarian. I'm sorry I haven't had the pleasure of meeting you yet."

His smile grew another half an inch with his introduction.

Yep, probably dentures.

I stopped, playing with the strap on my backpack. I hadn't come up with an excuse for my visit, but Mr. Everett seemed like he really wanted to talk.

"I'm Kate," I mumbled, still wrapped up in my mission. "I'm, uh, just browsing. Always looking for something to read."

"You sound a bit like Mrs. Everett." The librarian chuckled, turning his back. He returned a second later, grasping a gold-framed, black-and-white wedding photo from what I assumed was his desk.

The man in the picture wore an old-timey tux and thick glasses, similar to the ones Mr. Everett wore in that moment.

Beside him was a woman in a lacy, long-sleeved gown. The picture was aged and yellowed, but I could tell she was pretty. A veil draped over her black hair, woven back into a neat bun.

"Wow," I said, unsure of what else to say. "So, you're both into books, huh?"

"Oh, no. She always had me beat there," Mr. Everett creaked. "Lived with her nose in a book."

His smile faded slightly as he placed the frame back on the desk. "She passed away about ten years ago now. I was retired but took up this post about a year after I lost Harriet. Being around the books makes me feel close to her."

Gut punch. An old man who spent his days missing his wife? More like Up *than I thought.*

"I'm really sorry, Mr. Everett," I said. I wanted to stay a minute to make him feel less lonely, but the chill around me had grown stronger. Jane had to be in there somewhere.

"Oh goodness, don't be," he said, flashing those pearly whites in a wide grin. "I love it here, and I love helping you rascals. I'm here a lot, even outside school hours. Don't ever hesitate to let me know if there's something I can do for you."

My mouth parted, mirroring his giant smile.

How could anyone not love this guy? Sweeter than anyone Disney could dream up.

With a wave, I headed for the row of books furthest from the check-out counter. The shelves were lined with thick, blue encyclopedias. Mom told me that was how she had to look up stuff for her school assignments back in the day. They were dusty and heavy-looking.

Nah, I'll stick with the internet.

Jane sat with her back against the wall, reading her chemistry book. When she heard my footsteps, she glanced up and smiled.

"Thank goodness you're here. I hate ions." She stretched one arm as she slammed the book closed with the other.

I peeked back over my shoulder to ensure Mr. Everett wasn't anywhere close. I sat down across from her and whispered, just in case.

"You know you can read anything you want now that you're, uh…" I stopped myself. I'd let that comment slip out without any thought of how rude or hurtful it would be. I had been doing an awful lot of that lately.

"Dead?" she responded, copying my whisper. "Yeah, I suppose you're right."

Jane's smile remained, even after my impolite comment. "It's always felt important to me to keep my chem book close. I don't know why." She shook her head.

"So, how are you?" Jane added. "You seem stressed."

"Tired. Last night was… weird," I said in a lowered voice, unsure of how Jane would take the news. "I met with Millie. She isn't the villain we thought she was, but she did tell me a bit about what happened the day of the fire."

"Wow, are you serious?" Her eyebrows soared halfway up her forehead. "Oh my gosh, what did she say?"

I recounted Millie's memories of the exams and Mr. Davis's comments.

"I was going to chem tutoring almost weekly leading up to that exam," Jane recalled, her body seeming to tense. "I had no idea she was that embarrassed. Did she do something to get back at me?"

I continued my story with Jane hanging on my every word. I explained that Millie wasn't responsible for the fire. That she had done something, but Jane wasn't the target. When I told her about the phone line, she brought her hands to her mouth and her chem book dropped to the floor. Tears formed in her eyes, but I couldn't detect any anger in her expression.

I paused. "I'm sorry. I can't imagine what it's like for you hearing this."

"I remember that part," she muttered. "I remember trying to pick up the phone to call 911, to call the school office, anything. I assumed the fire had damaged the phone line or something."

Jane paused, apparently lost in her thoughts.

I did what I wasn't supposed to do and broke the silence.

"It doesn't excuse what she did, but Millie is still heartbroken over what happened," I said softly. "She said she never would've pulled that stunt if she'd known."

Jane's reaction caught me off-guard.

"I know. I'm not mad." She reached down to pick up her chem book and wrapped it in a hug across her chest. "I'm just overwhelmed. I think I feel sad."

I watched Jane work through her emotions. In only a number of days, her perception of Millie had changed in so many ways. She went from a competitive classmate to a murder suspect to someone who had prevented Jane from getting help on the night of her death—but she was paying for that sin every day. Jane finally spoke with a maturity that put mine to shame.

"What happened that night trapped me in here and trapped Millie in—whatever place she is now, emotionally. I wish I could give her a hug."

I couldn't believe what I was hearing. Even after the trauma of what she'd been through, Jane was still so genuinely kind. She felt deeply for others. I wanted to reach my arms out and give *her* a hug, but I'd already pointed out she was dead once in the conversation. I still didn't know how a hug would work.

"I ought to get ready for class, Jane. I promise I'm not giving up on you. I'm going to make this right."

Jane nodded, the edges of her mouth lifting slightly upward.

As I turned to walk out of the row of encyclopedias, something didn't feel quite right. Leaving Jane didn't feel right. I knew my nightmare was just a dream, nonsense from my brain working itself out. But if there was any shred of truth to it, the answers we needed were right in front of us.

How can we make ourselves see them?

Chapter Twenty Five

It was Taco Tuesday in the cafeteria. That pretty much topped the list of worthwhile things that happened at school that day. I caught up on some of my reading for Mrs. Marsh's class while I ate.

As I left school at the end of the day, frustration overwhelmed me. The answers Jane and I needed could be within arm's reach, but the investigation had no clear path forward. There was nowhere obvious to go to make progress. I found myself headed for home, like a normal seventh grader. Something I would do before I knew Jane.

When I got home, I sprawled my schoolwork across the kitchen table. I read a few chapters from my social studies book, then completed the worksheet Mr. Smith assigned us about circles and diameters. That stuff was so mind numbing. I thought again of Jane. She chose to continue studying schoolwork even after her death. I knew I wouldn't have the drive to do the same.

She would've been a really great doctor.

I willed myself to focus.

After homework, I heated up some ravioli from a can I found in the pantry. I ate it while I watched Mom's 6 o'clock broadcast. Unsurprisingly, there were no worthwhile headlines. Just a lot of hype from the perky weather guy about more rain later in the week.

I felt around the couch for my phone, finally grasping the hard case between two cushions. I tapped the email app. Buried beneath some junk mail was a message from Gwen.

> *Don't get either of us in trouble with this stuff.*
> *Glad I won't be on my own next summer. xG*

I raced past the part where she was apparently serious about making me her summer intern. Instead, I zeroed in on the favor she'd delivered. The state fire marshal's report was attached. My heart raced. I clicked on it. The document was labeled "Investigation Report." It was all very official-looking. Beneath the header were the details I already knew: the address, date, building name, etc.

My eyes searched frantically for one word in particular. Maybe it would be the word that would bring this whole investigation to an end and give Jane the peace she deserved.

Cause: Suspicious Structural Fire

I skipped a breath. There *was* something *suspicious* about the fire. Jane was right.

I frantically searched for the notes that would tell me what led investigators to that conclusion.

The notes stated that the building was unoccupied and locked at the time the fire broke out. They said investigators determined a Bunsen burner in the chemistry lab had been left on. They'd also identified steel wool at the scene.

I swiped out of the report to open my internet browser. I

searched "steel wool flammable." The pictures that popped up looked like a wiry sponge, and the words beneath them confirmed my fear. *Highly* flammable. I went back to where I'd left off in the report.

The rest was technical and filled with firefighter jargon, but from what I could tell, authorities confirmed from witnesses that paper decorations hung from the ceiling somewhere in the room. Based on the presence of the steel wool, the burner being left on, and the death of a child, the fire marshal's office labeled the incident as suspicious.

Think, Kate, think.

I didn't know why Jane was at the school that October night, or why she was in the chem lab in particular. Burners involve gas and open flames. They were obviously not supposed to be left unattended.

I flopped onto my back. When I landed on the couch cushions, it hit me like a lightning bolt.

Someone left the burners on on purpose.

I brought my gaze up to the ceiling, trying to draw mental notes above me to sort everything out. Jane's murderer left burners on in a chemistry lab. *Fact.* He or she had to have convinced Jane to come to the chem lab that night. To lure her into his or her trap. *Fact.*

My imaginary notes began to quiver. I felt lightheaded, forgetting to breathe as my mind raced.

I heard the front door creak open, and I released a loud scream.

"Whoa, kiddo, just me!" Mom shouted, pumping her hands to quiet me down. "It's been a slow news day, so I thought I'd drop in and surprise you. You're never going to guess who's been texting me!"

She sort of sang the last few words. She was giddy.

"Gil," I said sternly, my heart still pounding.

She walked into the living room. She wore a black work suit and heels. My indifferent response had dulled a bit of her shine, but she nonetheless plopped down onto the couch and tried to reach her arm around me.

"What's got you riled up? Are you not cool with me possibly seeing someone?" she asked.

"Oh my gosh, Mom. Not everything is about you!" I shot back. My tone sounded aggressive, but I was in the throes of an actual panic attack. I was closer than ever to catching Jane's killer. I brought my eyes back to my phone screen to be sure I'd clicked out of my email.

"Show me your phone," she demanded.

That wasn't like Mom. I stared at her.

"I'm serious, show me your phone."

"No, Mom," I said with a forced calmness. "We're better than that. Be normal and respect my privacy."

Her expression turned colder.

"You have a choice. Let me read what you're doing on your phone, or I'm turning it off and locking it in my safe for the night."

What the heck?!

I knew I couldn't risk Mom learning what I'd been investigating. She didn't let things go. She'd wear me down into telling her the truth, then she'd put a kibosh on it going any further. I couldn't believe I was about to take a real stand against my Mom. That wasn't us.

"Fine," I said smugly as I powered my phone off. I'd already read the fire marshal's report anyway.

Mom's jaw dropped. She snatched the phone from my hand, and her cheeks grew red with anger. She frowned.

"I don't know who you are right now."

My insides felt all twisty and gross. I wanted her to know the truth, but I couldn't risk blowing things. I was too close.

I watched as Mom opened the safe behind the bookshelf a few feet away. She dropped my phone in and locked it shut with a key that she dropped into her work bag.

"I want you to think about whatever it is you're not telling me —and if it's worth it," she said, as she picked up her bag and walked out of the room, her heels clicking against the wooden floor. "I'll leave your phone on the table for you in the morning."

I didn't respond, unsure of what I could say.

"Well, lock the door behind me," she said, resigned to my silence. "If you have an emergency, Mrs. Labott is home next door. You can call me from her house. I love you."

The door shut firmly behind her.

My head continued to spin. In fact, my interaction with Mom had only made the dizziness worse. The look of disappointment on her face had broken my heart. I reminded myself I was keeping her at a distance so I could help Jane, and it wouldn't be long until life went back to the way it was before. I focused on deep, slow breaths as I bolted to the bathroom. I grabbed a blue cup that sat next to the sink and thrust it under the tap. My lips parted to take a big sip. I was no help to Jane if I passed out home alone. I could never bear the stress of being a real investigator.

Once I'd drained the glass, I held the sides of the sink and faced myself in the mirror, watching my breaths flow in and out. I stood there until I could at least think clearly.

Without my phone to keep me company, I spent the rest of the evening reading a Stephen King novel I found in Mom's room. Its front cover was tattered, and its spine hung on by a thread. Mom was notorious for re-reading the same ten books until they basically fell apart. This book—*It*— was getting close to that point. Enjoying one of her favorites made me feel like crap for how I'd treated her. I read until my eyelids grew heavy.

Shaking my head to stir myself, I decided I should brush my teeth and wash my face in case I fell asleep. I changed into a cozy gray shirt and sweatpants, then returned to my spot on the couch. The exhaustion of the day and the fight with Mom had completely worn me out. It wasn't long until I was back in the chem lab, flames swirling around me.

Chapter Twenty Six

S moke once more filled my lungs, throwing me into a coughing fit. The orange and yellow flames danced around me, devouring one of the atom models overhead, then scurrying away, across the ceiling, and spreading. The whole room I'd come to know and fear was disappearing quickly.

Panic was unavoidable—but this time, the space, the horrible scene, was extremely familiar. I'd had enough of these nightmares by then to know there was no sense in screaming for help. No one would come. I looked to the small glass window in the door to be sure. No faces.

I took the deepest breath I could muster between coughs and willed myself to find my courage. I wiped what I assumed to be soot from my cheek, then began my trek around the room to any areas not yet devoured.

If this room held any additional clues about who killed Jane, I was going to find them. Ultimately, I would wake up from this nightmare drenched in sweat and coughing. But I was going to get out. In the meantime, I had to be brave. And I was armed with the knowledge that the fire started with a Bunsen burner in the middle of the room.

It was hard to know where to begin. I tried to shield my stinging eyes and marched to the front of the classroom. Just before the chalkboard, in the far corner, was Mr. Davis's desk. The front edge of it was engulfed in flames. A grading book dissolved into ashes. His name plate was blackened.

The heat got more unbearable with every step I took. Beyond the fiery wall, I spotted the desk phone with the cord cut, as expected.

I turned away and looked up to the ceiling. There had to have been at least a half-dozen atom models hanging down before the fire began. They were disappearing quickly. They resembled fire balls more than atoms. One dropped to the floor and sizzled.

It didn't seem like a giant leap. Fire from a Bunsen burner had ignited the steel wool. That probably threw sparks that hit one of the hanging atoms, causing it to catch on fire. It was fuel for the flames.

The air became blacker by the second, and my throat burned. I coughed again, choking on the smoke. The violent movement thrust my head and gaze downward, as I coughed into my hands. In a flash, I saw it out of the corner of my eye.

It couldn't be.

I dropped to my hands and knees to crawl across the floor around various burning objects.

Its edges were singed, and soot pooled in the binding where the pages met in the middle.

Jane's chemistry book. It was lying on the floor, open to a page titled Iron Oxide. There was a purple sticky note stuck to the page.

Its message sent me flat onto my backside. In a frenzy, I pushed back, frantically hurling my body away from it. Tears stung my eyes like the smoke stung my throat.

A scream escaped my mouth and sent me into another

coughing fit. I scrambled to get to the door. It didn't matter that no one was coming. I threw my fists against it, pounding and wailing with every ounce of energy I had left. I needed to get out. I needed the world to know I'd found Jane's killer.

At that moment, a chunk of ceiling tile crashed to the floor. One of the panels hit my head, knocking me to my knees. The impact of the hard floor sent a jolt of burning pain. I screamed again as I dropped to my side, grabbing at my legs. The flames drew closer to me. They were only a few yards away. Resigned to the same fate I suspected Jane felt that October night, I tried to calm myself. I prayed that something would wake me up. I grabbed for my charm bracelet and begged Bubbe to get me out of there. I had to tell the world the truth.

My eyes returned to the note on the chemistry book that was, by then, half burnt.

Chapter Twenty Seven

My body shot up from the couch with a gasp. All the flames around me had disappeared. The only light in the living room came from the faint glow of the TV. My gray shirt clung to me with sweat. I fumbled for my phone to check the time, then remembered Mom had taken it away earlier that night. The digital clock on the Blu-ray player said 8:42 P.M.

I was too stunned to process any of my thoughts.

Mr. Davis? How is it possible?

A teacher. A man trusted with the safety of people's kids. I felt sick. I brought my feet to the floor and rested my head in my hands, reminding myself to breathe and sort through what I could.

I'd known Mr. Davis was an odd guy, an unfriendly guy. He was kind of a loner and did things his own way. But being quirky was not a giveaway that someone was a murderer. He had fooled everyone around him for decades: students, parents, police, and even Jane's family.

I was reeling and needed answers. I needed Jane to know the

man she'd defended was the person who'd killed her. I also needed Mr. Davis to know that someone knew his secret. I couldn't risk the chance that he might hurt anyone else.

I looked down at myself, regretting my wardrobe choice. But I didn't have time to change. I needed to get to Jane. That meant I needed to get to school. Together, we would find a way to confront Mr. Davis.

I reached for my phone again.

Of all nights, it had to be tonight? I had to have some way to call for help if I ran into trouble. I processed my options for a moment but settled on Mom's tablet and threw it in my backpack. I figured in addition to having some kind of contact with the outside world, I could also keep an eye on her texts and other activities. I needed to beat her home.

If I was going to catch a murder suspect, as I'd intended to do with Millie, I would need evidence. I ran toward the stairs to get my GoPro that was charging in my room. But as I grabbed for the banister, I stopped.

I need to beat her home. What if this is the time I don't get to come home?

My lightheadedness returned, but I fought it back with a firm shake of my head.

Not this time. Tonight was not the night to feel sad or scared. I needed to be braver than the night I met Millie in the park. This time felt different.

I proceeded up the stairs and snatched the GoPro from the top of my messy desk. I placed it carefully in the front zippered compartment of my backpack. Then, I headed back into the hallway, walking the full length to the panel in the ceiling that led to the attic. I needed to find something to protect myself, and I had a feeling I'd find it up there.

I reached overhead and seized the string hanging from the ceiling. With a tug, the hole in the ceiling appeared and the ladder to the attic descended to meet me. I scurried up, rung by rung. When I reached the dusty room, I turned around in a circle, the wooden floorboards creaking beneath me. I hadn't been up there yet, but I knew Mom had. In the darkness, I extended my arm and searched for a string that would turn on a light. When I finally found it, I gave a firm tug. A faint yellow bulb clicked on. I didn't have to look long. Mom's pile of sports stuff was only a few steps away. I grabbed her old softball bat and stared at it.

Do I even know how to swing this thing? I figured if I needed a way to defend myself against Mr. Davis, I'd figure it out.

I sent the ladder back up into the ceiling and beelined downstairs for the last bit of protection I had time for.

I grabbed a sticky note and pen from the junk drawer. I scribbled what I hoped would be a note Mom would never read. Same as before with Millie. I hoped I could throw it away before she ever got home.

Mr. Davis killed a student named Jane Wright back in 1995. I've been investigating what happened, and now I'm off to prove it. I'm sorry I lied.

Not the most elegant thing I'd written, but again, I didn't have a single minute to waste. Grasping my backpack and the softball bat, I ran to the front door, glancing back over my shoulder one final time. Back in the kitchen, I caught sight of the note I'd left. It ended with the most important message I could ever leave for my mom:

I really love you.

Mr. Davis killed a student named Jane Wright back in 1995. I've been investigating what happened, and now I'm off to prove it. I'm sorry I lied. I really love you.

 KTRD

Chapter Twenty Eight

The streetlights were the only lights that shone as I approached Ravendale Middle School. All the windows were dark. Ghost inside or not, the school looked vacant and eerie. I slowed from a jog to a brisk walk, the softball bat in my hand CLUNK-CLUNK-CLUNKING against my leg with each step.

As I got closer to the building, it occurred to me I had absolutely no plan.

How am I going to get Jane's attention from outside the school? Do ghosts sleep?

I considered pounding on the school's front doors, but I caught sight of the school's security camera pointed at them. I had no alibi if security or police dropped by to check on the kid with the softball bat trying to break into the building.

That won't work.

I stayed on the sidewalk across the street and started a lap around the building, looking for doors with no cameras. I looked shady. I glanced over my shoulder here and there to be sure no one was watching. Thankfully, the streets seemed about as sleepy as the school. Or so I thought.

When I reached the back side of the building, the lights suddenly switched on through the stained-glass windows of the library. There was an old, rusted Buick parked at the curb. On the bumper, a sticker said "I Love to Read."

Mr. Everett.

I couldn't believe my luck. Without a second thought, I took off across the street, through the school yard, and to the doors that opened to the library. I had no clue what I might say to him. I hoped the words would come to me.

THUD.

The heavy door closed behind me. With some difficulty, a startled Mr. Everett pushed himself up from a cushioned reading chair in the middle of the room. The loud sound had caused him to lose his place. The pages of whatever thick book he was holding danced back and forth, as he awkwardly gripped its spine.

"Who's there?" he called out. The wrinkles around his eyes looked even deeper as he strained to see.

"It's Kate Sablowsky!" I crossed the library to allow him a closer look. "The new kid, remember? I was in here the other day."

"Ah, yes, Kate," he creaked, sucking in a deep breath. He grasped for an armrest on the chair and used it to lower himself back into his seat. "You gave me a bit of a fright."

I glanced around. The library was peaceful in the dark. Beautiful, actually. The only light came from above the check-out desk and two lamps near the center reading area. Everything else was shadowed and still.

"I'm sorry. I just, uh, forgot some things in my locker. From the street, I saw the light turn on. I hope that's okay." I gave myself a D+ on my story's creativity, but an A+ for luck. No matter what was about to happen, at least there was a responsible (non-murderous) adult nearby. "I could be a few minutes. Might knock out one of my assignments while I'm still here. I won't get into any trouble."

Mr. Everett adjusted his glasses as he listened. "Does your mom know you're here? And why do you have a bat?"

Crap, the bat.

"Umm, I was getting in some batting practice," I said. "Have to fill the time somehow while Mom's at work. That's why she doesn't know I'm here." That part wasn't a lie. I hoped that answer satisfied him, because I had to get to Jane—fast.

"Well, okay. Be sure you come back through here on your way out, so I know everything is alright. Harriet always said I was one of those pushovers." Mr. Everett chuckled and broke into a warm smile.

"Sure thing, Mr. Everett!" I shouted, already rushing toward the doors that led to the hallway.

What I saw next stopped my legs entirely, freezing me to one spot in fear. A strong and sudden chill shot down my spine.

Not again.

There was a figure in the shadows just to the left of the doors. A woman in an ivory-collared blouse, tucked into a high-waisted carmel skirt. Her pale skin almost glowed in the darkness. I was certain screaming wouldn't help me. All signs pointed to the fact that whoever it was wasn't *here* anymore. That meant shouting for Mr. Everett would do nothing.

Who is she? Does she know what I'm about to tell Jane? Is she here to stop me?

The woman took a step forward, toward the lamps' dull light. Her black hair glistened. It was pulled back into a neat bun.

"Edgar doesn't hear very well." Her voice was soft and warm. Her brown eyes were concerned, not angry. "I know you're here to help someone. I've felt that person here many times over the years. Please be careful."

It was then I remembered why her hair looked so familiar.

The wedding photo.

This was Mrs. Everett.

I couldn't respond without confusing or scaring Mr. Everett. Instead, I nodded and continued past her, through the doors, and into the hallway. I already knew I was headed into a dangerous situation, but I hadn't considered Mr. Everett probably wouldn't hear if I called for help. That wasn't a great feeling, but I didn't have much of a choice.

I jogged through the doors and away from Mrs. Everett's chill until I reached the seventh-grade hallway.

It was pitch black.

Even under different circumstances, the long, dark void would qualify as creepy.

"Jane! Jane, it's me!" I called out, still trying to sound hushed. I had no idea where Jane went at night. I took a few steps, using my bat to feel around in front of me. If anything or anyone was there, I wanted no more surprises. "JANE, C'MON!"

It was then I saw movement in the darkness. I couldn't make out much, but I was pretty sure I saw the pop of a stark white collar as a shape rushed toward me. Jane's blue eyes pierced through the blackness.

"What are you doing here?" she asked in a tone full of surprise. "How did you even get in here? Wait a minute, what's the bat for?"

Her nose crinkled in amusement.

"I'll get to that," I said, shaking my head. My heart pounded with adrenaline and focus. I was finally about to help Jane, for real this time. "You're not going to believe this. I think I figured it out."

Jane stared at me.

"You... what?"

"I know this is going to be really hard to hear, and I don't have any real evidence," I began, nervous about Jane's reaction.

"Go on, tell me! I'll be okay. I need to know," she insisted.

I leaned in close and spoke in a hushed tone. I hoped it would make the sting of the truth less painful.

"It was Mr. Davis."

And just like that, the secret wasn't my secret anymore. I watched as it sailed from my mouth to Jane's ears. My eyes had adjusted to the darkness well enough to see her standing in silence, shocked, as she absorbed the horrifying news.

"Mr. Davis?" Her lower lip began to tremble. "But we were so close. How could that be?" A big tear tumbled down her cheek and splashed onto her gray sweater.

"I know it doesn't make sense to you," I said. "It doesn't to me either."

I'd have to show her my lackluster proof. I rushed toward a hallway light switch and flipped it on to help us see. "Do you have your chem book with you?" I asked.

Jane nodded, another tear collapsing onto the cover, as she cradled it in her arms.

"This is going to sound crazy," I said, walking back to face her. "I had a dream a couple nights ago that Millie told me it was up to me to help you remember what happened that night. Does that make any sense to you?"

Jane's brow furrowed in deep thought. "No, I have no idea what you mean. I'm so confused."

"It was like Millie was telling me the answer was right in front of us this whole time," I explained. "Then, I had a different dream tonight. I know it was just a nightmare, but I think there was something real. I'm like my grandmother was. I can see things. Things other people can't. Like how I can see you."

Jane looked at me, seeming to try to put the pieces of this horribly complicated puzzle together.

"Flip through your chem book, Jane. Look for a sticky note. It's possible it's been buried in the spine of the book all this time, and you've forgotten it was even there."

Jane opened her book and began to carefully flip through the pages. When she stopped, I knew my nightmare had been right. Her eyes grew wide. She dug her pale fingers deep into the spine of the book and pulled out a crumpled purple sticky note. She shook as she worked the wrinkles out. Her mouth dropped open.

"Oh my gosh," she sputtered, as memories seemed to rush back to her. "I was with him that night. I was there for tutoring, Kate. I didn't tell my parents because I didn't want them to know I was struggling. What happened? Why would he want me dead? And why did he lie?"

Her eyes frantically searched my face and the air around her for answers.

I took a deep breath to deliver the news. "I think we need to ask him that ourselves. Tonight."

Chapter Twenty-Nine

I turned the handle on the chem lab door, but it was locked. I peeked through the thick glass window. With the help of that single hallway light, it looked like Mr. Davis's chem lab was asleep. Clean, bare, and dark. The room was so sterile, like a new chem teacher could move in the next day, and no one would think twice.

How can we get inside?

I wanted to walk around the space with Jane and see if we could trigger her memory. My scary-movie knowledge should've lent itself to picking locks or something, but I had no confidence I could make that work.

"So, what do we do?" Jane stood opposite me, fidgeting with that worn corner of her chem book.

"We need to get him here," I stated matter-of-factly, as I plopped my backpack and bat onto the floor. "And I think I have an idea how. When in doubt, I use my mom, the news lady."

I bent down and unzipped the backpack, pulling out Mom's tablet.

Jane's posture shifted with nervousness. "What do you mean? You're going to tell your mom about me?"

"No, no, no." I shook my head. "I'm going to make Mr. Davis think I'm my mom and that I'm onto him. I mean, if he thinks a story is in the works about his guilt, he'll show up. He's not dumb."

I flipped open the tablet's cover and pulled up Mom's email. All teachers' email addresses in Ravendale schools had the same formula. Last name.first name @ RavendaleIAschools.edu.

As I typed, Jane watched over my shoulder.

To: davis.jonathan@ravendaleiaschools.edu
From: msilver@ktrdtv.com
Received an anonymous tip about you. We need to talk immediately. Meet me in the chem lab, where it happened. I'm waiting.

I didn't bother with an email signature.
Do these kinds of demanding emails need signatures?
I racked my brain for movie examples of emailed demands but couldn't think of any.

"Here's hoping that worked." I sighed. "All we can do now is wait."

I deleted the email from Mom's "sent" folder, so she wouldn't see what I'd done. She probably wouldn't be keeping up with her emails that close to news time anyway. Then, I continued to refresh her inbox over and over again, in case Mr. Davis responded. I would need to read his email and delete it before she noticed or else this whole thing would be off. But what kind of murder suspect would send something in writing? He seemed like a lonely guy and probably watched his share of *Law and Order* episodes. He knew better.

"So, what's your plan exactly?" Jane asked after a few

minutes, pressing one of her hands against the glass window on the chem lab door.

I obviously didn't have one but explained that I would press record on my GoPro as soon as we heard any doors, any sound that could signal he was coming our way. As I spoke, I opened my locker and stuffed the threatening note card in my pocket in case Mr. Davis played dumb. Jane turned to look at me, concerned.

"Kate, I'm really scared," she whispered, her face as pale as ever.

"I know. This is your one real shot out of here. I'm not going to screw this up for you."

Her concerned expression told me that wasn't what she was referring to.

"You know you're about to face him alone, Kate," she said. My gaze shot up from Mom's tablet.

"*What?*" My stomach dropped. I couldn't believe what I was hearing. I was already a nervous wreck, and Jane was the only thing keeping me grounded. "Jane, I know this is hard for you, but—"

"I'm not *leaving* you, Kate. I'll be here, but remember Mr. Davis can't *know* I'm here. If you told him, he'd run. You need to get that confession from him some other way. None of us can leave without it."

She was right. I needed Mr. Davis to stay in one place long enough to confess what he'd done. If I failed, Jane could be stuck in this place forever.

BAM.

A door slammed, shattering the stillness of the empty Ravendale Middle School. He was here, and it was time.

Chapter Thirty

The sound of the slamming door bounced off the lockers on either side of us. From any outside entrance, it would only take Mr. Davis twenty seconds to reach the chem lab.

I shot to attention, punching the record button on my camera as firmly as I could. I shoved it in my backpack and left the compartment unzipped. Good video wasn't necessary, but the audio had to be clear. I set the bag on the floor so nothing could distract me.

I kept my eyes glued toward the direction of the sound. Armed with only a softball bat, I inched backward and positioned myself in front of my friend, spreading my arms wide to shield her from the approaching evil. Pounding footsteps filled the hall.

The only other movement came from particles of dust floating around us, made visible by the single fluorescent light above. The rest of the hallway was dark. I shuddered, thinking of what was about to emerge from that darkness.

"We'll be okay. Everything is going to be okay," I whispered to Jane, not believing my own words for even a second.

I listened as the steps grew closer. They belonged to a murderer. A killer who had stolen the life of a child and was now on the way to meet us.

When he finally rounded the corner, his gray hair was tousled. His tan windbreaker had a large mustard stain. This wasn't the robotic, straitlaced Mr. Davis I recognized. He'd left his home in a hurry. He pounded the hard floors with his big white sneakers as he came tearing down the hall.

When he saw me, he slowed his pace. His eyes narrowed in anger and confusion. He gave a furious push of his glasses up his nose and continued toward me.

"What is the meaning of this, Kate? You think this is a joke?" He spit out the words through gritted teeth.

My stomach dropped. I glanced at the bat in my hand then took a deep breath, forcing my eyes to stay as cold as his.

"I know what you did to Jane," I managed. My voice quivered slightly. I hoped he hadn't noticed.

It only took him another five or so strides to close the gap. I could see his hands trembling. He was only a few feet away. He may have been old, but he was still tall and relatively healthy. He wouldn't have any problem hurting me. The thought was terrifying. He opened his mouth to respond.

"That's preposterous," he said, actual wads of spit flying from his mouth in rage. "I have no idea what you're talking about, and I have every intention of calling your mother this instant." He fumbled in his pocket for what I assumed was his phone.

"Go ahead," I bluffed. He stopped. "She'll show up with a photographer and soon everyone in Ravendale will know the truth. That you're a murderer! Thanks for your stupid note, by the way."

I pulled the folded note card from my pocket and threw it at him. Adrenaline coursed through me.

Mr. Davis's face was flushed. His jaw clenched. Sweat ran down the sides of his face.

"Note? What note? I didn't write any—" he stammered before bending down to pick up the note card.

Mr. Davis's fingers shook as he attempted to unfold it. Any color he had left in his face drained completely as he read the message.

"I know you don't believe me, but I didn't write this," he said, almost pleading.

BAM.

Just like before, a door slammed, sending echoes down the hallway. My head snapped to look at Jane. She stared back at me with wide, terrified eyes.

Who could possibly be coming if Jane's killer was already here?

"You'd better not be planning any surprises, Mr. Davis," I shouted. I tightened my grip on the bat. "Who was that? Who just came in?"

Mr. Davis wiped his forehead with the sleeve of his windbreaker. He looked back over his shoulder toward the sound.

"I told her not to come," he whispered. "I told her not to do this,"

I couldn't tell if Mr. Davis was talking to me or himself.

Her?

"Jon? Jon!" a voice called out, as a shape emerged from the darkness.

A shape with curly, wild hair.

My heart sank.

The hallway lockers started spinning. I couldn't believe it. I knew the face I was about to see before it came into focus.

"Jon, I came when I saw your text. That you were coming here to meet the news people. What is going on?" Mrs. Marsh demanded.

Jane gasped, but only I could hear. Mrs. Marsh was the last possible person we could think of who would be involved in something like this. Yet, there she stood.

"Marilyn, I told you not to come," Mr. Davis snarled. "I can take care of this myself. It's all one massive misunderstanding."

Mrs. Marsh didn't listen. She extended her arm, blocking him from saying anything more. She stepped in between us. Her curly hair was gathered up into a messy ponytail, and her ears were naked without her signature dangly earrings. She wore a black hooded sweatshirt and black yoga pants, as if she had been sitting on her couch relaxing one moment, then running to confront a news crew the next. Like Mr. Davis, she hadn't had any time to prepare herself. Any glimmer of her bubbly, Mary Poppins personality was gone.

"Ms. Sablowsky, what is the meaning of this?" she pressed. "Where is your mother?"

Mrs. Marsh was deadly serious. I lifted the bat to the ready position to swing if necessary. She took a step backward in response, horrified.

"Don't come any closer," I shouted. Now wasn't the time to let up. "I don't know what you're doing here, but I know Mr. Davis lied about leaving early to help his mother the night Jane Wright died. I know Jane was with him in the chem lab for tutoring. He rigged the Bunsen burner so the room would catch fire!"

I glanced at my backpack, praying my GoPro was doing its job.

Mr. Davis stared back at me, his mouth hanging open in shock. Mrs. Marsh was, too, but she spoke calmly, nonetheless.

"Our mother," she replied.

"What?" I gasped. I wavered as the hallway continued to spin.

She took a step toward me. "I said, *our mother*. Jon is my brother."

One of my hands dropped from the bat and came to my head, trying to get the spinning to stop. It was possible I was going to puke in the middle of the hallway.

They're siblings? Did they do this together?

Sensing my confusion, Mrs. Marsh continued. "You are entirely incorrect in your belief that Jon killed anyone intentionally. That couldn't be further from the truth. What happened to Jane Wright was my fault."

Tears formed in her big brown eyes. She wiped one away with the back of her hand.

"That's not true, Marilyn, and you know it," Mr. Davis scolded. He dropped the wrinkled note card as he brought his hands to his face. Heavy sobs erupted from his shoulders. He stepped backward until his back rested against the lockers. He slid down until he was seated on the floor, curled up with his knees against his chest. It was the least put-together a person could look. Mrs. Marsh watched him crumble and slumped down beside him.

"It was a terrible accident," he sobbed.

What is happening? Why are they both confessing to being responsible for Jane's death? And yet they claim it was an accident?

The bottom line was, I'd caught Mr. Davis in his lie. I had no clue what Mrs. Marsh had to do with anything, but what good was stalling? It was uncomfortable to see two grown adults cry, but I clung to my bat, willing myself to stay strong. I zeroed in on Mr. Davis.

"What, I'm supposed to feel bad for you? Jane died *alone* in your chem lab after the tutoring. You've been lying for decades. You expect me to believe her death was an accident?"

He didn't raise his eyes. They stayed plastered to his palms.

"I thought I'd turned the burner off. We finished our session. Jane *promised* me she was within minutes of heading home. I locked the door behind me out of habit, like I do every day. It never occurred to me she wouldn't be able to—" His sobs cut off his sentence. "Oh, God, I'm so, so sorry!"

I was at a loss for words. Mr. Davis was falling apart. Mrs. Marsh wrapped her long arms around him as he wept.

What is going on?

Jane drew closer, pulling me from my foggy state.

I turned to look at her, not caring what either of the teachers would think if they saw me acting strangely. Tears streamed down Jane's pale cheeks. She nodded. The past was coming back to her. I couldn't believe it, but her eyes said Mr. Davis was telling the truth.

I moved an inch toward the crumbling mess of a man before me. Like Millie, he wasn't a monster. He was an old man who had finally unloaded a secret he'd carried for years. Still, there was more to uncover. I sat down across from them, setting my bat aside.

"You locked the door behind you, like you do every day," I reiterated, trying to wrap my head around what he was telling me. "You didn't realize you'd locked her in."

Mr. Davis lifted his head. His face was red and tear-stained. Mrs. Marsh kept him tight within her embrace. Her cheeks were tear-stained too.

"Yes. I've always wanted to know why she didn't just call for help." His eyes searched for answers.

"Well, the phone line was cut," I said calmly, quietly, before I could catch myself.

"What? I didn't do anything to the phone, I swear!" he shouted in disbelief as another wave of panic overtook him.

"No, no, Mr. Davis, I know," I said. "It was Millie Jefferson. She was upset about her bad grade and tried to get under your skin."

Mr. Davis's brow furrowed. Mrs. Marsh leaned closer to be

sure she'd heard me correctly. Neither of them understood how I knew what I did, but I didn't have time to explain it to them.

"You said you thought you'd turned the burner off, but you hadn't. Why was it on in the first place?"

Mr. Davis wiped his eyes again with the sleeve of his windbreaker. He stared straight ahead as he recalled what I assumed was the worst night of his life.

"We were doing a unit on iron oxide. It involved heating steel wool on the edge of a ruler. We'd completed the experiment, and Jane was taking notes. She assured me she was almost finished but didn't want to slow me down from getting home to Mother. I've gone over that night again and again, every night since. Jane must have tried to repeat the experiment, but something went wrong. The steel wool probably sparked. Maybe she shook the ruler, I don't know. She must have been so scared."

Mr. Davis hung his head in shame.

"The flames caught those decorations you had hanging from your ceiling," I said with understanding. "Even if they weren't right above the lab tables, they weren't far away. That must be why you're the only teacher who doesn't have any personal touches in his room. That's why you keep things so... empty?"

He nodded.

"I couldn't risk anyone else getting hurt," he said, still staring forward.

"So, why lie?"

Mr. Davis sighed. At last, his eyes met mine.

"I had just started my teaching career," he said. "Mother had so many medical needs, so many bills. If anyone had found out my negligence led to the accident, I would have lost my job." He paused.

"It was a choice I made at the time. A stupid choice. And I've paid for it every day."

"So have I," Mrs. Marsh agreed. I'd been dying to know what role she played in all of this.

"What exactly did you do?" I asked her, seeing a glimmer of her caring personality return to her face.

"Jon would never have been put in a position to teach full-time and care for Mother if I hadn't left him to pursue a writing career in New York City," she said, tears continuing to flow. "I'd abandoned my big brother in his time of need. He made one mistake, and a girl lost her life."

This time, Mr. Davis wrapped his arms around her.

"I came home as soon as it happened. I took a job at Ravendale the following year, teaching English so I could be here to support him. I knew after a tragedy like that, he would never be the same. That's why I left you that note in your locker. When you started asking questions, you had no way of knowing who you could be hurting."

Mrs. Marsh turned her gaze back to Mr. Davis. "And Jon, you haven't been the same. We can't keep this secret anymore. We just can't."

She buried her face in his shoulder and sobbed.

I was at a loss for words. Neither of their stories made what had happened okay, but it made them human. Their pain radiated through the hallway.

Jane crouched down next to me.

"Tell them I'm okay, and I'm not mad," Jane said. "Tell them I forgive them."

Mr. Davis must have noticed me staring at nothing. He tapped on Mrs. Marsh's shoulder. Both regarded me with puzzled eyes.

"Are you okay, Kate?" Mr. Davis asked.

I took a deep breath.

"This is going to sound crazy, but Jane wants you both to know she's okay. She isn't mad at you, and she forgives you."

I cast my eyes to the floor, unsure if I wanted to see their reaction to my nonsense.

"She—forgives me? Us?" Mr. Davis asked in disbelief. "How do you know?"

"I just do, okay?" I shot back defensively, as I pushed myself up to my feet. "I don't think I'm going to tell anyone what you did."

Mr. Davis shook his head. "It's not your burden to bear, Kate," he said. "And Marilyn, it's not yours either. *I* need to make this right."

Chapter Thirty One

Ten Months Later

A drop of sweat ran down my forehead from the heat of the early morning sun. I welcomed the air conditioning as I scanned my key card at KTRD and pushed open the doors. There was no guilt, no nerves. I had permission to walk there by myself.

"Well, if it isn't my little workhorse," called out a familiar, nasally voice with a head of perfect braids from behind the desk. "I need ten copies of these files, stat."

Gwen's long red nails pinched the documents as she plopped them into my hands.

"For crying out loud, Ms. Gwen, let me put my stuff down first," I said with a laugh.

"It's not even 9 A.M., and you want me to start reminding you how much you owe me?" she asked, with a big heap of attitude.

This was our dynamic, and we both grinned.

Gwen was right though. I did owe her after all the favors she'd pulled to help me last fall. She cashed in on my offer to be her summer intern as soon as school let out. I claimed I regretted it, but really, I didn't. Almost three weeks had passed, and I was having... fun.

I slumped my backpack on the floor and trotted over to the copier to crank out Gwen's copies. I smiled as I glanced back at Gwen's desk. Her son, wearing his Vikings sweatshirt in the framed photo on her desk, smiled back at me. Gwen pointed out the picture of Trey several months ago when I came by the station with Mom. She didn't say much but told me he died when he was thirteen. I'd recognized his face and fade hairstyle almost immediately. Trey was the boy who'd followed me the night I met with Millie. I'd seen him around town a few other times throughout the year, but he was shy. Occasionally, he would smile, but he mostly kept his distance. He seemed to like checking in on his mom though. One time when Gwen went to the restroom, I told Trey I'd be here whenever he was ready to talk. He avoided eye contact but mumbled "thank you" in response. He hadn't taken me up on that offer yet.

He wasn't the only ghost I occasionally spotted around Ravendale. I'd seen Mrs. Everett twice more since the night we confronted Mr. Davis. Both times, she was reading near Mr. Everett—once at the school library and once while he read at the diner. It was no wonder he was able to sense her presence around books. That's where she usually was.

"Been meaning to ask you," Gwen said, snapping me back to reality. "Have you heard anything around town about that teacher of yours? The one who left? Got another call from a viewer asking about him yesterday."

Gwen's nails tapped against her keyboard as she talked.

I sighed. "Nothing since the last time you asked."

I hadn't seen Mr. Davis since that night in the Ravendale Middle School hallway. I guessed that was the benefit of having such an empty room. It wasn't hard to pack everything up and disappear.

To everyone else in Ravendale, Mr. Davis's departure was shrouded in rumor and speculation. But I'd heard the story straight from Mrs. Marsh. Well, Marilyn. She said I could call her that when other people weren't around. We were bonded forever over that bizarre night in the seventh-grade hallway and what followed. Mr. Davis turned in his resignation to the school the next day, then he tried to turn himself in to the police for lying in their investigation. The officers hadn't seen much point in pursuing charges twenty-some years after the fact when the fire was accidental. Mr. Davis paid Jane's parents a visit before packing up his house and putting it on the market. He was long gone before the sale was final. Like a ghost, he'd truly vanished.

Mrs. Marsh asked me to stay after class one cold winter afternoon.

"He asked me to thank you," she said. "He said he doesn't know how you figured out what you did, but because of you, he's okay now."

I assumed that was a reference to what I'd told him that night: that Jane was okay. It was our secret, just the three of us. Mrs. Marsh never elaborated about where Mr. Davis went, and I never asked. But sometimes, in class, I caught her watching me. When I returned her gaze, she smiled. Naturally, she'd returned almost immediately to her giddy, Mary Poppins self. I wasn't wrong in my initial assessment that she deeply cared about me. Maybe after that night in the hallway, she cared even more.

With one last beep, the copier spat out Gwen's final copy. I tapped the sheets against the countertop so all the pages aligned. I handed them back to her.

"Anything else for me, your majesty?" I asked sarcastically.

"I'm sure I'll need a coffee at some point." Gwen winked. "But for now, go type away at your screens like you kids do."

Being Gwen's intern meant a lot of "me time," since she was one of the least demanding people in the world. I was super grateful for that. After the year I'd had, I needed some time to decompress.

One way I was doing that was starting my first screenplay. I was probably too young for any formal screenwriting class, but the format of everything didn't matter. I needed to express what had happened between Jane and me in my seventh-grade year. It was a spooky story but one that had what I hoped was a peaceful ending.

The truth was, that night in August was the last time I ever saw Jane.

After Mr. Davis and Mrs. Marsh had gone home, Jane walked me to the furthest part of the seventh-grade hallway before the turn that led to the library. We kept a distance from the library's doors, so even if Mr. Everett's ears were working exceptionally well that night, he wouldn't hear what he would assume was me talking to myself.

"Kate, I feel lighter. I don't know how to explain it, but I don't feel weighed down here anymore. I think I'm finally able to leave, and it's all because of you." She took a step closer to me. "I told you that afternoon in the library that you were great in your own right. I meant it, and I want you to remember. I think you're going to make a difference for lots of others in the future."

The chai charm on Bubbe's bracelet tickled my wrist. Even if Jane was right, I couldn't go there. Not right then. My best friend in Ravendale was about to leave me.

"So soon?" I asked her, trying to sound braver than I felt. "Where are you going?"

"I don't know. I want to see my parents one more time, even though they won't be able to see me." Jane paused. "Then, all that's left is to pass on. I have no idea where that is or what that is, but honestly, I can't wait to find out."

Despite her cheerful tone, there was still a sadness in Jane's eyes.

"Is... everything okay?" I asked.

"Well, you've done so much for me," she said. "But there is one more thing."

I stared back, giving her my reluctant permission to continue.

Jane's lower lip quivered. "I'd feel a lot better if my parents *knew* I was okay."

I knew I wasn't comfortable yet with anyone knowing I had Bubbe's gift. That I could talk to ghosts. Especially with the people who were grieving the ghost I'd gotten to know. But Jane needed me, one last time.

"How about a letter? Let's write it together, like that paper for English class," I offered with a small smile.

I got a blank piece of paper from my locker. We sat on the hard, cold floor of the hallway under that single fluorescent light, writing what we thought would be the right amount of truth for Jane's parents without overwhelming them. Our sentences were to the point.

Dear Mr. and Mrs. Wright,

You don't know me, but I'm a student at Ravendale Middle School. I know this sounds crazy, but I'm friends with your daughter, Jane. You probably don't believe me, and frankly, I don't blame you. If it helps, Jane told me you used to call her Buttercup. She pretended to hate the nickname, but she actually liked it. In fact, if you look under the desk in her room, she carved the nickname into the bottom of it. She said you should go look if you don't believe me.

I'm only bothering you because Jane wants you to know she's okay. She's sorry she lied about going to the diner. She was really getting chem tutoring but didn't want you to worry she'd fallen behind. Until recently, Jane was still here. She needed to know what happened to her. Together, we learned that what happened was a terrible accident. Now, she is headed someplace better. She doesn't want you to feel sad anymore.

I'm not quite ready to share who I am yet. But some day, when I am, I promise to tell you everything. Until then, please know Jane loved you very much.

—Jane's friend

I folded the note and put it in my backpack. A quick check of my phone showed I had less than a half hour to beat Mom home. I gathered my things, and knew all that was left was to say good-bye. I felt my throat tighten.

Jane noticed, which was so like her. Always thinking of others' feelings. She extended her arms out to me, her pale skin glowing. Despite how I'd felt mere days ago, I didn't care what weird or spooky sensation I was about to experience. I needed a hug from my friend.

My arms wrapped around her thin frame. Jane's chill flowed through me, like stepping outside of a heated store into the winter cold. My fingertips went numb. My body stiffened as the freeze seeped deep into my bones. Still, I didn't want to leave. Her cold-yet-trusting grasp made Ravendale feel like home.

"Thank you," she whispered.

"I'll never forget you, Jane," I responded, as I slowly pulled away.

I bent down to pick up my thankfully unnecessary softball bat and took a few steps toward the library's wooden doors. A quick peek over my shoulder showed Jane was already gone. She was gone from my life as quickly as she had come.

I delivered the note to her parents' mailbox after school the next day. Since then, I'd walked by their home at least once a week, wondering when I'd feel ready to tell them our story. It hadn't happened yet, but I knew each day was another day closer.

As my days at the station passed, I typed away at my screenplay, telling the story of the girl with pale skin in the gray sweater. And the movie-loving, sarcastic girl she'd chosen to be her friend.

"Hey, kiddo!" a familiar voice sang out from the hall that led to the newsroom. It must've been 2 o'clock when Mom's shift started.

"Hi," I answered back, slamming my laptop shut. I didn't want Mom to see my screenplay yet. Of course, by then, she knew most of the details of what had happened that fall, but I still didn't want her proofreading my stuff. She could be such a bossy editor.

The day after Mr. Davis left, I told Mom about Jane. I told her I had Bubbe's gift, and Jane had come to me for help. I even fessed up to the bits about going places without permission and meeting adults after dark. She was not happy about that part. I apologized for being shady about my phone and not telling her the truth.

In her classic style, Mom's reaction was one of concern, not anger. She shared with me that Bubbe discovered her gift when she was about my age. She said Bubbe used to struggle with it, that she was often afraid and had nightmares. It helped to know what I'd felt was normal, if anyone could call seeing ghosts normal. She promised to back off a bit in the future if something "gift-related" was going on and I said I was okay. I promised her I wouldn't lie moving forward.

"What do you say we walk to the diner after the 6 o'clock news for dinner?" Mom asked. "Gil has enough staff to cover, so he can join us. Maybe if Sam is free, you could invite him along too."

Mom and Gil had been officially dating since the fall. They dropped the "love" bomb sometime around Hanukkah. If Ravendale had an "it" couple, it was them. The whole idea of Mom being mushy with a guy was puke-worthy, but she was really happy. Plus, Gil and I got along well.

I hadn't been sure if I'd make any real connections in Ravendale, aside from Jane and Gwen. I still texted Bailey every so often, but honestly, I texted Sam more than anybody else. Like he'd hinted when he saw my *First Full Moon* shirt, he loved horror movies. Together, we officially launched Ravendale Middle School's film club, even though we only had a few members. Sam still said goofy, awkward things now and again, but we cracked each other up. We'd actually become pretty good friends over the school year. I hadn't told him the truth about Bubbe's gift or Jane yet, but I had a feeling we'd get there.

"Sure, Mom. I'll text him," I said with a smile.

"Sounds great. You're a keeper, kiddo." Mom's perfect blond, TV waves barely moved as she turned around.

If anyone would've told me when I moved to Ravendale, Iowa, that I'd enjoy my life, I would've said they belonged in an asylum like the one in the movie *Halloween*.

But there I was. And I had found a way to make a real difference.

Maybe my walk home from dinner that night would lead past the Wright home. Then again, maybe not...yet.

Life's not just the here and now.

THE END.

Are you ready for more of She's Still Here? Check out the Monarch website www.monarcheducationalservices.com for the She's Still Here Reader's Guide. This free educational resource is perfect for educators, librarians, homeschools, small groups, and readers who want more of Kate's story.

Acknowledgments

People always want to know where the ideas for books come from. This one started on the floor of my kids' playroom. Amid the clatter of toys and toddler babble, I asked my husband a series of "what if" questions. *What if there was a sarcastic girl who moved to a small town? What if she had a mysterious classmate at her new school? What if she had her bubbe's ability to see the dead? Ability? Nah, there must be a better term for that.*

Before long, the story of Kate and Jane took shape.

Thank you, first, to my treasured publisher and friend, Dr. Jen Lowry with Monarch Press. Your belief in this spooky story made this possible. Thanks for lifting up your writers and only ever being a quick text away. You are a blessing to me and so many others.

Thank you to my fellow authors at Monarch Press. I love the house that Jen's built.

Thank you to Kelly, Sally, Kara, and Haley for challenging me to make this manuscript the best it could be. Each editing round was a privilege, and I learned so much from you.

Korin, you are an incredible talent. Thank you for my beautiful cover art and your careful attention to detail.

Eric, thank you for your feedback as I crafted my fire scenes. Journalists like to fact-check things, and you were very patient with me!

Chey and Wendy, thanks for the name inspiration!

Thank you, Meg, Tom, Lynn, Amy, and my "Gossip Boys" for

reading early drafts and helping me talk my way through this thing.

Thanks to the online writing community and groups like #MomsWritersClub for your advice, guidance, and support. Additional thanks to my sensitivity and ARC readers.

Leon, you're one of a kind. I gave you a one sentence pitch of this story, and you've never looked back. Thanks for everything.

Mom, Dad, Britt, Jess, Nessa, and Coach, thank you for your love and encouragement. (Sorry you had to read horror, Mom!)

Perhaps my biggest thank you goes to my husband, Ian. Thanks for listening to me on the playroom floor that day and every day after that. For reading countless drafts. For helping me work through tricky scenes. For believing in me when I didn't believe in myself. You are the best partner I could have ever asked for on this journey.

Lexi and Landon, my favorite part of waking up is being your mommy. I hope you see parts of yourselves in these characters and in other books you come across in the future. I love you so much.

And finally, thank you to you. Thanks for buying this book, borrowing this book, sharing honest reviews online, requesting this book at your library, and spreading the word about it. However you found SHE'S STILL HERE, I'm glad you're here.

About the Author

Caitlin Alexander is a children's author and award-winning journalist. She loves uplifting young girls through literature, ghost stories, and sweet treats. Caitlin lives with her husband, two beautiful children, and pup in southeast Minnesota.

Our Monarch Collection

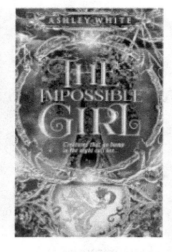

If you know someone is hurting or if that person is you, please reach out. Talk to school staff, family, and/or a friend, and reach out for professional help if needed. Know you are not alone. You are loved.

National Suicide Prevention Lifeline: 988

Crisis Text Line: Text "Hello" to 741741

National Alliance on Mental Illness (NAMI) www.nami.org

National Center for PTSD: www.ptsd.va.gov/